T0169194

The Third Person

The Third Person

stories by
Emily Anglin

BookThug · Toronto, 2017

FIRST EDITION

Copyright © Emily Anglin 2017

The production of this book was made possible through the generous assistance of the Canada Council for the Arts and the Ontario Arts Council. BookThug also acknowledges the support of the Government of Canada through the Canada Book Fund and the Government of Ontario through the Ontario Book Publishing Tax Credit and the Ontario Book Fund.

BookThug acknowledges the land on which it operates. For thousands of years it has been the traditional land of the Huron-Wendat, the Seneca, and, most recently, the Mississaugas of the Credit River. Today, this meeting place is still the home to many Indigenous people from across Turtle Island, and we are grateful to have the opportunity to work on this land.

All rights reserved. No part of this publication may be reproduced or transmitted in any form or by any means, electronic or mechanical, including photocopying, recording, or any information storage or retrieval system, without permission in writing from the publisher.

LIBRARY AND ARCHIVES CANADA CATALOGUING IN PUBLICATION

Anglin, Emily, 1979-
[Short stories. Selections]
    The third person / Emily Anglin.

Short stories.
Issued in print and electronic formats.
Softcover: ISBN 978-1-77166-366-3
HTML: ISBN 978-1-77166-367-0
PDF: ISBN 978-1-77166-368-7
Kindle: ISBN 978-1-77166-369-4

    I. Title.

PS8601.N47A6 2017   C813'.6   C2017-905402-3   C2017-905403-1

PRINTED IN CANADA

For Rose and Alexis

The Third Person:

EILIDH

EILIDH WAS A SCIENTIST. AND LIKE MOST OF THE SCIENTISTS I meet in my job as a support-staff member at the Mind Institute, she was a scientist with a problem.

When she appeared one morning in the doorway of my office in the basement of the Arts building, I rose to greet her with a slightly startled welcome. We'd agreed by email to meet at this time, but I was still surprised to see her— to see anyone. I'd become conditioned by identical days of desk work on the summer-quiet campus, in the dim of my concrete office, to expect as my only company the overhead footfalls and shouts of the summer-camp kids who ruled the floor above mine, which served as home base for the Institute's annual neuroscience-themed day camp. Eilidh's sudden, full-grown presence in front of me made me feel like I'd been caught sleeping.

"Eilidh," she said, introducing herself. I gripped her hand, almost bracing myself against her solid stance. Her palm was hot. "Sorry I'm so out of breath," she said. "I rode my bike here." She held up her helmet, showing me.

I repeated her name in my head as she'd spoken it: I-lee. Not eyelid. I'd been reading it phonetically, I realized, despite knowing how the name was pronounced. Likewise, I realized I'd been picturing her as a slip of a person, the bodily match for the polite but spare email she'd sent me to ask for an appointment without saying what she wanted to meet about. In person, she turned out to be tall, athletic, broad-shouldered. Beads of sweat stood on her forehead despite the basement chill.

"Hi, Eilidh," I said. "Come in. I'm Miranda."

Eilidh set her things down on the floor and dragged a chair for herself from my office's back corner; she placed it at an angle near my own chair, as much beside as across from me, as though we were meeting to work on a project together. Recently, all my work had been done over email, or occasionally by phone. I hadn't had an in-person meeting in months. Eilidh, by contrast, seemed at home in the room, as though accustomed to meetings with strangers.

"Nice record player," she said, as though she were visiting me for fun. "And nice record."

"Thanks," I said. "I like personalizing my workspace." On one of the wall-mounted bookshelves, I'd placed a record player on which I liked to play ambient music at the lowest audible volume. An eclectic set of carefully selected records sat beside the player between heavy, polished brass bookends in the shape of owls. That day I had a classical-guitar record playing. I'd read a professional advice book once that said it's a good idea to move homey things into your office, things of your own. I have the privilege of feeling quite secure in my job, not least because my father was one of the Institute's founding scientists and is still affiliated with the Institute as an emeritus researcher, but I still thought it couldn't hurt to soften the space with some personal touches.

Essentially, I work at the Institute as an advisor. My job description has changed several times in the five years I've worked there, but my title has stayed the same, broad enough to encompass the various roles I've played, some at the same time: Personal & Professional Wellness Specialist. The awkward phrase is a symptom of my position's compound nature, the collapsing of jobs held by separate people into one role: but essentially, I help our scientists talk through professional development plans, career goals, work-life balance, resources for wellness, and other related issues.

At my interview for the job, my hiring manager, Rick, had opened the interview by telling everyone about my master's degree in counselling psychology. He told the other interviewers that I'd followed in my dad's footsteps by building my life around the study of the mind—"Miranda's dad's name is a big deal around here, as I'm sure you all know," he'd said. I'd gripped the seat of my chair on either side of my legs. Rick made a joke about how he had grown up to become his dad too, but would need to get his own psych degree before going into that.

The Mind Institute was founded by a progressive group of psychologists in 1962, in what was then a near-pastoral setting of fields on the city's eastern outskirts. This group broke off from the psychology department of the city's major university because of that department's emphatic refocusing away from the paradigm of inner states and toward the certainty of outward actions. The secessionists hoped the pastoral scene would foster a new humanistic, interdisciplinary approach to studying the mind, and they recruited scholars from the natural and social sciences, and even the arts, to join them.

More recently, in its current incarnation, things had been tense at the Institute, between funding cuts and the increasingly frequent emailed security alerts detailing irregular incidents taking place on the Institute grounds, which were desolate by night.

And I needed the job, which I'd applied for shortly after my father's retirement. My dad had been the youngest of the Institute's founding psychologists, and only a doctoral student at the time, twenty-five years old. The Social Psychology building is named for him, and still bears his name on the sign out front. He lives with me now—it's just the two of us. We spend evenings together, talking while we watch documentaries on public TV, and he tells me things that the documentarists leave out. I tell him about goings-on at the Institute. He likes to hear about the camp kids running around, playing a game called Mind Maze, run by the weary counsellors outside, though he can't quite understand why the kids are there, and seems to think they must be participating in a study of some kind.

Eilidh didn't look like the typical Mind Institute researcher. In the chair beside me, she was turning through her notebook in search of some notes she said she'd taken that morning. I opened my own notebook and wrote the heading "Meeting," followed by the date.

She must be new, I thought. There was an air about her that seemed imported from an early-1990s tennis match. She smoothed her loose, straight beige skirt against her legs. She wore a striped navy-and-white short-sleeved top. She still looked sweaty. She dragged the back of her hand across her forehead to push her bangs aside, and I focused more closely on the one incongruous element of Eilidh's otherwise conventional appearance: her streaked, heavy, silver-grey eye makeup. She must have unknowingly smeared the makeup when she wiped the sweat from her face during her bike ride—riding along in the margins of the hot, wide streets, the back of her wrist swiping across her face as she pedalled, her other hand holding the handlebars steady, her eyes trained on the east, unaware of the makeup spreading along the lines around her eyes.

It must have taken her hours to get to my office. Why ride all that way in the heat just to meet with me? For a moment, the thought of this physical effort made my job feel more important.

The guitar record had finished playing. I sat up straight to listen to what Eilidh had to say.

"I didn't want to talk about this over the phone or email," she said. She crossed one leg over the other, resting her elbow on her knee and her chin in her hand. Three simultaneous folds.

"This is going to sound weird. I know that. But I just have to start talking, and we can work from there. I have a problem, and it relates to my work, and my research, but it's also personal. The problem is that I've developed an obsession with looking. I'm obsessed with looking," she said. "I know that's not very clear, but could we try to start there?"

I moved my chair back a bit, trying to find my bearings, and considering, quickly, where I'd draw the line, and what mark I'd use to say the conversation had gone outside my job description, as it might, if it got too psychological. If things stayed vague, it would be hard to say who the appropriate support person should be. My job was broad enough that I did many things, but for that reason it was important to me to draw clear boundaries where they could be drawn. I'd listen and assess.

She filled my office with the smell of watermelon juice mixed with water. I reached for my glass and drank. Water serves in my windowless office as a surrogate for breeze.

"Okay. Absolutely," I said. "Maybe to get us started, we can chat a bit about what you mean by 'obsession.' And by 'looking.' Does that sound like it could be useful?"

"Of course," she said. "I'll try to be as open as I can, but I also don't want to predetermine your thinking about me. Basically, by obsession I mean that I feel unable not to do something."

"Hmmm. That could be closer to a compulsion, but I think I see what you mean."

"Maybe," she said. "Either word is fine with me."

It was at that moment that I realized that her makeup hadn't been spread by a careless rub, but instead may very well have been applied deliberately and asymmetrically: a metal-grey streak above one eye, and above the other, a thick, metal-grey, slightly curved line drawn about an eighth of an inch above the lashes, like a pre-plastic-surgery incision mark.

Oh, no, I thought, in a warm rush of anxiety. It couldn't be that her grey eyelids were some kind of reference to her name's phonetic pronunciation. Or to her problem with looking. Or both. Could it? I decided to pretend for the time being, even to myself, that the thought hadn't occurred to me.

"And what kind of 'looking' do you mean?" I asked.

"I'm not sure I should name that. Not that I want to make this difficult... I don't at all, and I'm so grateful for your time... and your professional opinion. I'm grateful that there are supports here, people like you to help us with the complicated jobs we do, as sorry as I am that I'm sure that makes your job complicated too."

"Well, I'd like to help, if I'm equipped to. Or at least refer you to someone who can."

"I don't mean at all that I want to play games here. But I'm afraid if I tell you too literally what's happening, it will shape how you see me. It's not a comment on you, it's just something I've noticed about the way people think about other people. Would it be okay if we just say for the sake of the conversation that I have a compulsion to look over and over at myself in the mirror? It's not that at all, but it would give us an anchor for the conversation, like a placeholder."

"Sure," I said. "Maybe this will help... So far, what I'm hearing is that you're ready to think through this issue, and about how moving past your preoccupation or compulsion might help you to live and work better. I know you rode all this way up here by bike to see me, so your commitment to moving forward on this is clear."

I was trying to fill the hole in the middle of our exchange, to make things, at least emotionally, concrete, even if they had to stay opaque on the information-gathering level.

"Oh, the bike ride really isn't that bad. I don't mean it isn't a challenge, but it's really more the psychology of it than the terrain that takes a bit of taming."

Can psychology be tamed? Inevitably, it's something I think about quite a bit, working where I do, and living with my dad as I do. He still thinks about it too, even though he's retired, and far from the life he lived when he was working. Work was like home for him. Sometimes he still speaks in the assured, intent voice he used to use when talking about his work, when we're sitting together.

My dad's interests are encyclopedic, and of course include the history of the Institute itself. It's natural that brutalism, the architectural school that generated the Institute's buildings from the early 1960s, is another topic he likes to talk about. The name comes from the French word *brut*, or 'raw,' referring to raw concrete, the basic material, my dad might begin, during dinner or while we sip tea or wine afterward. But it means more than that too.

The Institute had started as a single, dome-shaped, submarine-like building of poured concrete in the centre of a broad meadow. Specimens of this meadow's flowers still hang pressed and framed on the concrete halls of the building I work in. The cheerful flowers appeared almost comical to me in the otherwise grim setting, until I saw that they were meant as a serious bit of institutional history. The Institute's halls look designed, not to cure the haunted mind, as my dad has pointed out, but to confront it through imitation, an aesthetic vision so open to interiority that it verges on daring. The buildings seem to consist only of interior space, even on the outside. Now, just the architecture of its founding era remains, a body unsuited to the new mind it houses, which looks up and out rather than down or in.

The Institute has a new nerve centre: the one contemporary, non-brutalist building, built the same year my dad retired. The new building is tall, airy, and its aqua-coloured glass glints in the sun. Once it was built, the president and other top brass were moved from their concrete towers to the new building's upper floors. Most of us at the Institute just call it 'the new building,' even those of us, like me, who started after it was built. Its actual name is the Innovation in Studies of the Mind Centre—its acronym, the ISM Centre, is an in-joke on campus, among some, as its researchers refract their academic thinking through the lenses of novel isms, from neoliberalism to motivational cognitivism. The glass it's built of makes it look transparent compared to the box-like concrete rectangles around it, but the aqua glass is tinted so that you can't see through it past the reflections of clouds and other buildings.

I often hurry to get away from the Institute after work, rushing when I'd rather linger and walk around among the ivy-twined concrete buildings and wild grasses rustling in concrete planters. The staff all leave quickly, because of the security alerts sent out by the Institute's president's office by email: most recently, the reports have described accounts of people being encircled by groups of unknown individuals. There's no good reason to risk staying after sundown.

"What kind of a scientist are you?" I asked Eilidh. I hoped it didn't sound like a challenge; it was an honest question. It was important to know. Plus, I was made uneasy by the thought that her eye makeup was some kind of coded message, and I was still trying to get a read on her.

"Social," she said. "I'm a social scientist. A social psychologist, more specifically."

"And what do you study?" I asked. My dad had also been a social psychologist. This connection meant that her office was likely in the building named after him, the building bearing my last name.

"Group consciousness," she said. "It doesn't help that I'm a loner, let me tell you. The irony isn't lost on me. I spend all

17

my time theorizing about the giant network of a brain we share, how we move together like a sea of birds." She put her hands out in front of her before folding them again, as if she was tempted to angle them together to illustrate the movement of birds but thought better of it. "But I'll do anything to get away from other people. For the last year, I've even developed a habit of coming to work at night, in the evening, or very early in the morning, so there's no one else here but me. Some people are good at sharing: I'm not like that. I can only give. Giving is very different from sharing. It's selfish. 'Give' is what I do with my ideas, my work. 'Take it all,' I might as well say. 'It's no good to me if it's part yours.'"

"What do you make of that? Have you come to understand why?" Eilidh's opacity seemed wilful.

"Sometimes I think giving is a substitute for sharing. A way of erasing immediate company, those directly around us, to achieve access to the shared mind, the big mind. You can only hear the shared mind from a place of quiet."

"Can you say a bit more about that?"

"Oh, I don't know if I should, or even if I can. For this conversation, it's enough to say I have a lot of trouble collaborating. I can link collaboration on paper to the collaborative thinking my science explores, but I myself don't collaborate. I look."

"In the mirror...for the purposes of this discussion."

"Yes, we'll go with that."

"And what do you see when you look in the mirror?"

"A door."

"You see a door?"

"Oh, no. Sorry. That's not what I see, but a door is part of the problem. Part of what my looking is about."

"What does the door symbolize for you? Where do you

think it might lead if you reached out and turned the handle?"

"That's the problem. It doesn't open. I should clarify. It's a real door I'm talking about. I can be direct about that. A real door that's locked, holding a space I can only look at and never enter."

"Where is this door?" I asked, still unsure if she was speaking metaphorically or literally.

"It's here, at the Institute. Like I said, I've been coming to work at night, and sometimes when I need a break I go out wandering, walking around, sometimes at three or four or five in the morning. The Institute and its grounds are so beautiful late at night. Have you seen it? In the dark, you can see how this place has gone back to nature. The flowers and weeds shine in the moonlight, the concrete crumbles, the ivy holds the buildings up. The architecture here is astounding, but we just step around and through it. Have you ever noticed all the unused spaces—the sunken courtyards? The staircases stacked on top of each other? The outdoor landings the size of ballrooms? The balconies, dry moats, gardens that are underground and open air at the same time? The fountains and pillars? This style of architecture was meant to make people congregate, and when you're alone in it, you can feel the power of the idea when it was in its pure form, before anyone knew it was bound to fail."

Her words made me recall my dad saying that the brutalist vision had been conceived to echo and encourage the ways groups of people move, to make them come together, but that it had failed disastrously, creating spaces that people could only stare at. "It's as though by thinking too long and hard about the problems that keep people from coming together," my dad had said, "the architects managed to capture not the way people congregate, but the isolation of working on a project that isn't really succeeding."

When I was young, we would walk around the campus together, and he would point out the odd features and details to me. I'm not sure if I would have noticed them as an adult if he hadn't, since my tendency is to stay focused on my daily tasks when I'm at work, seeing only the steps ahead of me that need to be taken.

"I haven't seen the Institute at night," I said to Eilidh. "I'm nervous being here after dark because of the security alerts. I don't mean to worry you, but we should talk more about that, before you leave, or another time soon. Let's not forget. But for now, about the door. Where is this door?"

"One night I was walking past one of the buildings—I'm sure you know the one; it has the rose garden built around it—and I noticed a light glowing behind a shrub at the building's foundation. I looked closer, and spotted the top of an outdoor stairwell. The entrance to the stairwell was overgrown, but I climbed into the garden and pulled some branches away. It was a steep, narrow staircase leading down the outer wall of the building's basement. I went down the stairs. At the bottom, there was a door set in the wall, completely covered with ivy. I stripped away some of the ivy and tried the door, but it wouldn't open. I pulled more of the ivy away and looked through the bars. The door leads to a courtyard. I know it all too well, even though I've never been there."

I felt uncomfortable. "The Institute is full of so many unused spaces, isn't it? I've noticed that."

Actually, one day after I began working at the Institute, I'd been looking for a rag to dust my office with, and had opened what I thought was a broom closet at the end of the hall. I had found a room full of old furniture stacked in piles: desks, chairs, decorative '70s textiles pulled tight across wooden frames. But also more personal things, things that you wouldn't expect: boxes of letters and books; a large, jumbled box of old shoes and hats; a box of what looked like homemade children's costumes. I closed the door and forgot about it.

"You know what?" Eilidh said. "Just saying this all out loud has already helped. Thank you so much. I think I know what the next steps are for me."

"But I haven't done anything. I want you to know I'm perfectly happy to keep talking, if you'd like. I'm here to listen. It's my job, after all. And we should also talk about safety before you leave."

"Thank you, thank you so much. But I really should get going." She stood up, collected her things. She slipped around the door frame and was gone.

After she left, I went back to work. It was late afternoon before I noticed that Eilidh had left her notebook behind on the corner of my desk. I gazed at it in my late-afternoon torpor. In the lower right-hand corner of the page she'd left it opened to was a little line drawing, a sketch of some of the buildings clustered around mine, including what I recognized as the Social Psychology building. A small rectangle was labelled "Stairwell to Courtyard." Beside the stairwell, a larger rectangle, contained inside the square of the building, was labelled "Courtyard," and on the inner wall of the courtyard, lines spaced at regular intervals marked out a hallway of smaller rooms. They had been labelled "Offices Looking onto Courtyard," including one that said "My Office."

I left the office later than usual. It was already starting to get dark. I always try to leave just before dark, with the security alerts in mind. The plan hinges on hurrying, shortening the transitional time between places, to allow more time for each place, each state, and less for the difference between them. But tonight, I'd pushed it. When I packed, locked up, and left the building, the light near the bottom of the sky told me that I had about fifteen or twenty minutes left before dark.

I came to the building from Eilidh's drawing. The sign outside read "Social Psychology," following my dad's name. This was the building where his office had been, and where Eilidh's was now.

I climbed over the garden to step into the ivy-lined concrete stairwell. Just like Eilidh had said, there was a door standing at the bottom of the stairs, a tall ironwork door set into the wall, with ivy recently torn away from it.

The door stood open, and its lock stuck out at an angle, as though it had been prised. I went down the stairs and inspected it.

There was a plaque on the bars that must have dated back to the '60s. "The Garden of Myth," it said in calligraphic script, and then: "Please enjoy this statue garden. You are welcome to this place of reflection."

I pushed the door open and stepped inside the courtyard. Three of its walls were pitted concrete, and completely overgrown with ivy that stained and gripped the grey surface. The fourth wall, opposite me, was glass, the wall of the Social Psychology building, behind which lay a bank of basement offices that looked out onto the courtyard through their thick windows. The offices were all dark.

Placed at regular intervals within the courtyard were short concrete pedestals, each affixed with a plaque. I walked from block to block reading the plaques. "Narcissus," said one. "Oedipus." "Prometheus." "Medusa." They must have once held statues.

I faced the pedestal where Medusa had stood. She would have been positioned to look into the office furthest to the right. I peered into the office, making out bookshelves and chairs and a desk, wondering what poor soul had sat in Medusa's line of sight when the statue still stood. As I looked, the door inside the office opened, and a tall figure stepped in, removing a pale scarf while entering and throwing it on the back of the chair. I could only see her silhouette, moving around and then freezing in place, as she spotted me. It was Eilidh. She turned the light on in her office and the courtyard was illuminated by the glow. She gave me a brisk smile and a wave, and then sat down at her desk and began writing by hand on a pad of paper. Was she just going to sit down to work like this, I thought, with me standing out here watching her? But she stood up and pressed the paper against the window and waved me over. I read her note:

"I opened the door. Now I can work again." Then, under it, in larger, loopy writing, she'd written: "P.S. The workday is done now! It's time for you to go home." She smiled. I nodded, but then shook my head a bit, as though to say, "Not sure."

I waved to her and headed toward the stairs, as though we were cubicle-mates in a shared office saying goodnight at the end of a long workday. I could tell she felt our meeting and what we'd talked about was wrapped up now, our project done, our collaboration complete. Her need was met, and I supposed my job, at least as it involved Eilidh, was also done. I felt in my legs how tired I was as I went up the concrete stairs, and wondered if I should just sleep in my office to benefit from the cool of the basement, to save myself the long ride home, and to allow for an early start the next day. And to resist the insistent order, from the president's office, and now from Eilidh, to go home, to never linger, to draw a line to step over between this place and the rest of our lives, as though that line would make things clearer and hold things apart.

I looked around at the campus like I'd never seen it before, among the summer evening sounds of cicadas and the voices of people coming out in search of the cooler air. Small clusters of people were gathering on the grounds at varying distances, talking, eating, like the area was a part-time park—an empty space in need of use. I wandered toward the bus stop.

TRYING NOT TO WORRY

SEVEN MONTHS AGO, MY MOTHER LEFT OUR FAMILY home and moved into a room in a stranger's house. She said she had found the room through a sign posted in the house's window. She also said, shortly after moving in, that her new housemate, Rosalind, is strange. More details came out during a difficult family conversation a few weeks after she left. One of these details was the possibility that Rosalind was what some people would call a sociopath, because of her unfixed personality that you couldn't quite get a handle on— her shifting, flat surface. But I still can't quite recall which of us had offered this reading of her based on the information my mom had offered.

Nonetheless, my mom says she's never been happier, so I'm trying not to worry. There's never been anything flat about my mom. She's faceted. She's lived separately from our family before, and has worked at a number of jobs, some of which have taken her far away from us from time to time, but in all her comings and goings, she's always been on her own except for us. No other name was ever mentioned as a co-habitant or companion, at least, until she told us about Rosalind.

I still live at home, even though I'm thirty-two. In the eyes of some, my story should probably be about my own kids by now, but at this point it's still about my parents and their kids. Since my mom left to move in with Rosalind, I live with my heartbroken dad and my older brother, Glen, who is also heartbroken, which is why he also lives at home: he just got divorced. Now I'm the woman of the house.

My dad still loves my mom, and she says she still loves him. She tells me they aren't divorced, not like Glen and Kali are. "He has no reason to worry. I love him just as much as he loves me. Actually, I'm quite sure I love him more than he loves me." It's about space, she explains. Not love or the lack of love.

Up until just recently, my mom and I would talk on the phone a few times a week, and chat about how my work is going, and how Glen's doing. She would tell me about her new place with Rosalind, but I wasn't gaining much of an understanding of who Rosalind was. It might be because I hadn't asked her much about it. I'd been withdrawing, thinking about how I needed to plan my own next step toward some kind of life for myself outside the house I'd grown up in, inspired by my mom.

"I'm okay," I'd offer, when she would ask me how I am. I'd curse myself as I said those closed, cold words, staring at the flesh of my forearm, picturing the words for what I was appearing there letter by letter, in the shaky script of a self-inked tattoo: "Traitor. Fraud. Failure." I'd rack my brain for a word that means all three.

"I still love your dad," she tells me. "And all of you. Why should Housing always necessarily be one of Love's departments anyway? The bureaucracy is ready for restructuring. I'm still right here."

I work part-time at the university teaching Victorian literature and composition, when courses come up that no one else can teach. When courses come up at universities in nearby towns, I drive there to teach them. Our family lives in a mid-sized university town surrounded by small to mid-sized university towns within about an hour's drive of each other. In the summer, the cornfields of the surrounding countryside roll in wavy hills toward groves of distant trees that dot the banks of small rivers.

I moved away to do some of my degrees, but I came back to this place and its somehow constant aural backdrop of flapping and cawing from crows that gather in large groups in the trees around the university. My students don't know that I still live in the house I grew up in.

My dad works at the university too; he's a psychologist. He started out in a relatively conventional area, with studies that analyzed how accurately people imagine the lived experiences and inner lives of strangers. But as his career developed, his research took a sharp turn into experimental and theoretical territory. He's become best known for conceiving of a theoretical phenomenon that he and his lifelong collaborator, Georges, have termed "spontaneous subjectivity transfer": a phenomenon whereby an individual becomes aware of a sudden, visceral understanding of another person's felt experience of being alive, an understanding that comes from out of nowhere—a kind of physical, automatic empathy. As they describe it, it's essentially as though one person's consciousness gets instantly thrust into the body of a stranger, to become part of their lived memory or understanding. The person experiencing this spontaneous empathy may know the person whose subjectivity they receive—or they may not know them at all; they can receive the subjectivity of someone who lives in the same city, or someone who lives hours, even continents, away.

My dad and Georges have done over two thousand interviews, compiling a database of scientific evidence for the phenomenon. They get called "occult" but they say there's nothing occult about what they see as a newly discovered form of intersubjectivity.

It's always been hard to tell what my mom really thinks of their work, despite the key role she played in its development. It was actually she who first brought the phenomenon to my dad's attention. A colleague of hers at the public library she used to work at had experienced something strange, and had confided in my mom about it.

As she explained it to my mom, my mom's colleague had been lying in bed one night and suddenly became aware of thoughts running through her mind—and feelings attached to those thoughts—that she didn't recognize as her own: she felt aware of a different body, one not lying down but standing, pressing against a wet kitchen counter, washing the dishes; she felt the rigidity of this other woman's body; she could feel this woman worrying about her son, until her worry pushed her to leave her house to go out looking for him in the rainy night, down distinct streets.

The colleague had told my mom about this, and had shown her the sketch she'd drawn of this unknown woman's house and the street names she'd seen. My mom, in turn, shared this story with my dad, whose curiosity was piqued. He and Georges did some investigating, and they discovered that this woman really existed, at a house matching the woman's sketch and description. They started doing some new studies, and found an avalanche of other examples, named the phenomenon, and began to build their career on investigating it.

A few years after this original experience came to light, my dad and Georges founded a research centre for investigating spontaneous subjectivity transfer; they've run it since then from the basement of the Social Sciences building. A plaque on their door says, "Understanding Is a Relationship," a line my mom came up with, and which I often think about. It's more complicated than it sounds. The lines of the plaque are etched in the metal very finely, so that you can hardly see them: at first the plaque looks blank, like a decorative metal rectangle, until you shift from one foot to another and the light catches the grooves.

My dad and Georges thank my mom in the acknowledgments sections of their books for typing and editing all their manuscripts. But as a family we acknowledge—if not in words, then simply through knowing—the more complex contribution she made to their work.

My dad and I have the same name at our workplace: we're both "Professor Rosin." But I tell my students to call me Nancy.

My students seem to feel comfortable asking me questions, maybe because I'm young. "Did these writers even want us to read their books like this? Didn't they just want us to read them for pleasure, like how we watch TV or movies now?"

"That's a good question," I say. I tell them about the crowds of people that would throng at the docks on the morning a ship was due to arrive bearing a new installment of Dickens's latest novel, some of them stampeding and some disappearing into the waves.

"Then why do we have to talk about themes?" they ask. "Why would you want us to do this? Why would you want to do this?"

I ask them what they come to know about other people through their own reading, watching, and listening. I become more and more aware of how little I actually know about the students or their lives—what responsibilities, work, worries they carry—and the fear of making assumptions makes me almost faint, as I try to tell them in various ways that I believe love and art are all we have. When my voice grows thin I let them talk to each other; I sit on my desk nodding and writing notes, as though I'm jotting insightful summary observations that will tie everything together, until I let them leave early.

I had been in the habit of talking to my mom about my classes at the kitchen table, after I'd gotten home and she'd returned from the doctor's office where she'd been working as a receptionist for the past few years. One such night, we were drinking tea together and my mom told me she had found an affordable room for rent and had signed a lease.

It's spring now, damp and echoing, and the air seems to expand at dusk, full of a diffused rain that cleans your skin as you walk. My mom called me last week and asked me to meet her at a café about halfway between our homes—between my family home and the home of Rosalind. Over coffee with some kind of orange liqueur in it we talked about how she'd been. She'd been calling me and asking to get together, but I'd been preoccupied with job applications and some copyediting work I'd picked up—a grant application some friends of mine in another city were putting together. But I was happy to see her.

"I just go out, walk around, feel the sun. I come home when I want. All I have to do is avoid Rosalind on the way to my room, if I don't feel like talking. I close the door, and the room is mine. I can lie down and close my eyes and rest."

"But what about Rosalind? What's her story?"

"She's unlike anyone I've met. At this point in her life, she's a bit...unmoored. I think people find her hard to understand. I don't see her reaching out to others in a conventional, overt way, from what I've observed, but I also know she's been through a lot. To be honest, I find her personality relaxing. She's calm. I'm here, and she's over there. She's not too close to see. She's unpredictable, but somehow she's also known to me, like a book I read a long time ago."

"You can read her like a book?" I paused. "Not like books where charming sociopaths are interesting rather than dangerous, I hope?"

"I don't think I know what a sociopath is. But the key is that I can read her. I'll always be able to get out of the way when I need to be away from her, and she needs to be away from me."

"'Get out of the way'? I'm picturing Norman Bates coming through the shadows. Should I worry?"

"Try not to, honey. It's important. Ask yourself: do you know what it's like to be me, or Rosalind, or your brother? And I'll ask myself the same thing. We all feel for each other, but that doesn't mean we know. Besides, where did this term 'sociopath' come from?"

"In general?"

"No, specifically. Well, in general, too. But I meant as applied to Rosalind."

"I thought you said it," I said. But then I remembered the

scene of the kitchen table on the night my mom had told us more about Rosalind: my brother Glen slumped over with his head in one hand, in front of a glass of whiskey; my dad's hands folded on the table, as though pinning it down to keep it from flying off; my mom looking tired, explaining Rosalind's personality and what she likes about her. I supposed any one of us could have thrown out the word 'sociopath,' and it could have just stuck.

When I came home that night after coffee with my mom, around nine-thirty, I saw that my dad had fallen asleep on the couch in front of the TV, where an old black-and-white movie was playing. The remnants of a dinner of toast and peanut butter sat on the coffee table in front of him.

Sometimes when I think about my dad's work I feel an impotent frustration well up in me that I can only express to or at other people. Why psychology and not sociology? It's fine to think about individuals, I think to myself, or tell Glen or my mom, but what about the systems?

But my dad works hard, and I was worried about him too. I tucked a blanket around him on the couch and called upstairs to Glen to ask him if he wanted to go have a drink.

"So, what are we supposed to make of this?" I asked Glen that night. "Just tell me what you think, and I'll argue with what you say until we figure it out. But I can't start."

We were sitting at a bar we go to a lot because it's close to our house: Fiddler's Dell. The lonely men and occasional women who frequent the bar tend to sit in silent solitude, except for a few quiet words tossed sideways now and then. There are green-upholstered booths illuminated by low-hanging lights. It's always dusty in there, in a way that makes it feel like a lined nest. Sometimes when Glen and I go for a walk together at night, without saying anything out loud, we just automatically walk toward it, go in, and order glasses of beer. The beer is usually stale, but the waitress brings a basket of pretzels, and it's a quiet place to talk.

There's one waitress who thinks Glen and I are married.

"It's good to get away from the kids for a bit. It's important. Time for just you," she said once, with the kind of sideways wink that always strikes me as a ballet of social grace. How could we begin to correct her or explain? Would we call her back to the table to tell her? Bring it up when she returns to check on us? Would she sit down with us for a while to talk about it? It would be too strange. Maybe it wasn't important for her to know the truth.

Besides, it was true, in a way, what she said; we did need time for just us. Glen and I are very close, although he's older than me—my parents adopted me when he was six. Our minds work together, room and anteroom. I always want to be with him, but then when I'm not with him I notice that my thinking becomes clearer; it might be because we drink a lot when we're together. He drinks a lot more than me, though. Oddly, Glen claims that it wasn't his own drinking, but someone else's, that caused his marriage to break down.

Unlike myself, Glen had his own house for a while—when he was married to his wife, Kali. Not long after they got married and bought the house, Kali asked Glen if her twin brother Andre could move in with them, because he was having a hard time. He was drinking himself to death, Kali told Glen bluntly. How could Glen argue with that? So Andre moved in.

But having Andre there was too much for Glen. He couldn't shake the feeling that Kali and Andre were criticizing him telepathically while he was in the room. And never once did Glen see Andre have even a sip of alcohol; he soon found himself wondering if Andre had made up the story about his drinking, or if Kali had made it up. Glen made the mistake of telling Kali his suspicions. "He's an alcoholic and you're upset because he's not drinking?" Kali had asked.

Glen started having night terrors: he would wake up yelling, and Kali said she couldn't help but feel like he was yelling at her. Things disintegrated from there, and Glen came back to us, about six months before our mom moved out.

"What I can't understand is how she's paying for the rent at the new place, since she's also helping me out so much," Glen said, his face softened by shadows in the dim light of Fiddler's Dell. He'd aged a lot in the last year. He wasn't working, though no one had told my dad that because Glen didn't want him to know; my mom had been helping him with lawyers' fees and some other expenses from what she made working at the doctor's office. "The place is really nice. It can't be cheap. Say what you will about Rosalind, but her house is beautiful."

"Mom does okay at the doctor's office," I said. "She's been working a lot, or at least she was up until recently."

"But they have a whole house to themselves."

"Rosalind's house, not hers," I said.

"Can we talk about Rosalind? Have you met her yet?"

"No," I said. "Have you?"

"Yes, I have, and the weird thing is that I liked her. Despite the worrying conversations we all had when Mom told us about her."

"But isn't that how sociopaths work? They're charming when you first meet them, but it's a veneer?" I said, wondering how I knew what I was saying.

"I know, but she just didn't seem like a sociopath to me. She didn't seem flat. I didn't really find her charming...just calm and pleasant. She was lying on the couch reading a novel with an afghan draped over her. I looked at her face while she was reading. She looked thoughtful."

"Did you see what she was reading?" I asked. It was irrelevant, but I was curious, looking for any window to look through to see who this woman was.

"I did look, but her hand was covering the title," he said. "If she was reading, though, maybe that means she's fine, and not a sociopath. To read you have to have an interest in others and an inner life, right?"

"I guess so," I said.

"Unless she was pretending to read. Or reading a book about getting ahead or manipulating people," Glen said. "Like Machiavelli's *The Prince*, or whatever the modern version of that book is."

"I doubt she was reading *The Prince*," I said.

"No, that's not really a lying-down read—it's more of a desk read," said Glen.

"Why are you making this into a game?" I said.

"I'm trying to distract you, and part of me is scared. It's how I cope. I'm sorry. But in any case, Rosalind seemed like a nice, calm person to me. Maybe there's something strange, but she may just be calm and nice."

"Then why is Mom implying that she's unmoored?"

"I guess that's the question. I think maybe Mom is just trying to say that Rosalind has been though a lot, and she's trying to get us to stay away and let them have their space. She doesn't want us trying to poke holes in her story. Besides, I don't think Mom ever used the word *sociopath* herself, come to think of it. I think maybe Dad did, or you did."

"I didn't call her that," I said, thinking that Glen himself may even have been the one who had introduced the word. "And I wasn't trying to poke holes in her story. I was just worried about her. Worrying and poking holes are different things," I said. Even as I said it, I began to worry it wasn't true—maybe when we worry about people, at least sometimes, we're really trying to unravel them, to integrate their selves with ours so we have more control. No, I thought. Worrying is part of love; only a sociopath wouldn't worry.

The next afternoon I let my students leave class early after a discussion of *The Woman in White* that I was having trouble focusing on. I decided to stop in at my dad's office to say hi. I walked down the muddy hill between the Humanities building and the Social Sciences building and went through a dented brown metal side door that led to the basement. A pipe dripped a rusty brown hole into the concrete floor inside.

I knocked at the door to the research centre, but there was no sound from inside. I brushed some dust from the plaque on the door, rubbed my finger over the shape of the words.

"Hi, Nancy," said a voice behind me.

"Oh, hi, Georges," I said, turning, my heart beating quickly. Georges was always so quiet. It was as though spending his life in a basement had soundproofed his body.

"Have you seen my dad?" I asked him. "Is he in today?"

"No, he hasn't been in at all this week. I know things haven't been great. He mentioned your mom has someone new in her life."

"He put it that way?" I asked.

"A woman came by here the other night, actually. I thought it was your mom, at first. She came in from the rain and she had a coat on, with a hood. But it was someone else, asking for your dad. I wondered if it was your mom's new friend."

"But my mom wasn't with her? Where was she?"

Georges unlocked the office door and turned on a lamp just inside it, on a desk. I stood on the edge of the threadbare carpet on the office floor, which was worn so thin that its pattern of squares and roses looked like it was painted right onto the concrete. It had been there since I could remember, an old carpet my mom once had in her bedroom.

"Would you like to sit down?" Georges asked. "I could make tea."

"That's okay, thanks. I should get home. I'm worried about my parents, actually."

"I know things must not be easy right now."

"No," I said. "I'm fine, actually." I couldn't open my mind to the merest threat of scrutiny through Georges's academic lens, even though I knew he was expressing concern as a family friend and not as a researcher. I pulled the door closed behind me and studiously avoided looking at the "Understanding Is a Relationship" plaque.

When I got home, this time it was Glen passed out on the couch. The TV was off, but the radio was on: it was tuned into a local AM station. A woman with a reedy voice was singing about following a river's song to the sea. Glen still had his shoes on, and they were wet; there was a smeared line of mud, still wet, beside one of his feet on the couch cushion. His face looked flushed and radiant. I knew he looked like that when he was very drunk, the same way he had looked as a kid when he had a fever.

I'd noticed that Glen had been drinking a lot—even more than usual. He'd been a heavy drinker as a teenager, but had seemed to pull things together as a young adult, until things got hard for him in the last few years. If we had a bottle of wine with dinner and started a second, that second bottle would always be empty the next morning, rinsed out and set on the back porch to be recycled. The bottles of bourbon, vodka, and scotch—even the liqueurs—in the cupboard dwindled quickly. My dad didn't really drink, so I knew it must be Glen. Looking at him, I wondered, not for the first time, if the story of Kali's brother Andre's alleged drinking problem had been cover for the role Glen's own drinking played in the end of his marriage. Kali had called me once, before the whole Andre thing, and asked me if I thought we should do something to help Glen with his drinking. We decided we would try, but were never really able to find a way of broaching it, and around that time he seemed kind of fine again for a while, until things got bad again, right before they separated. Not for the first time, I felt frustrated with him, and unsure of how much I could trust him.

"Glen," I said. "Have you seen Dad? Apparently, Georges hasn't seen him at work for a week."

"He's in bed," Glen said. "He says he has a cold."

"More importantly, apparently a woman came by, looking for Dad at his office, but Mom wasn't with her. This is getting weirder."

One eye opened slightly, but didn't quite look at me.

"Just because they live together doesn't mean they're together all the time. If you're worried, we could just go see her at the house," he said. "It's the big white house beside the train tracks. On Wallace Street."

"That white house? Why didn't you tell me? I thought you said her house was nice." The house on Wallace Street had stood empty off and on for years, with a sagging porch and windows covered over with ivy. As kids, we would stop on our way home from school and play on a tire swing hanging from a birch tree in the side yard, scaring each other as we swung back and forth by saying we'd seen someone move in one of the house's windows.

"It's fixed up now," he said, even as his eye rolled back in its socket. He was asleep.

I sat beside his legs on the couch and shook them. He wouldn't wake up. I turned the radio and the light off, and left Glen a note on the coffee table telling him I'd gone to Wallace Street to talk to our mom and Rosalind, and that he could join me if he wanted when he woke up. I let myself out the back door, noticing a cluster of phosphorescent green rings of light gleaming from the line of empty bottles sitting on the porch's floor, catching the beam of the street light overhead.

I walked around for a while in the rain before I turned onto Wallace Street and headed toward the white house by the train tracks. It was a tall brick house with what looked like a new roof and windows. The broad white wooden porch had also recently been repaired. Thick shrubs grew up on either side of the porch, reaching almost as high as the balcony that sat on the porch roof. Ivy, in places, choked the bricks, and in other places I could see the dried suction cups and twining stains left behind where ivy had recently been stripped away. The house was a full three storeys, with one light on in a second-floor room, behind curtains.

On the porch, I rang the doorbell and looked at my watch. It was just after ten. Too late, really, to come by unexpectedly and still act casual about it, but I didn't care. I rang the bell again, and waited. I walked back out to the sidewalk and saw that the light in the second-floor room was off now. I thought about it and decided that if my mom lived in the house, it was fair game for me to open the door and look for her. I went back to the porch, opened the screen door, paused for a second, and then tried the door. It swung open, and I was looking into a carpeted front hall, with a dark kitchen to the left ahead, and a staircase leading upstairs directly ahead of me. I stepped in quickly so that I wouldn't have time to think about what I was doing.

But as I started up the stairs, which were lined with family pictures—people posed in groupings, individuals sitting portrait-style—the candid smiles of strangers in their quaint, multi-picture frames made me realize I'd essentially just broken into a stranger's house and was walking up into that person's private world. Though I was filled with fear—for myself, but also fear *of* myself, this reckless, aggressive self—the need to see and know pushed me forward, no matter the consequences.

I got to the second floor and called hello—but no response. There were more pictures along the wall and the faint sound of a TV. Then a door, and a hallway at the end of which I heard a whirring sound mixing with the TV voices behind a final door. As though compelled, I knocked on the door, preparing to face the shock and anger I deserved for being there uninvited.

Nothing for a moment, then the door opened. It was a woman a bit younger than my mom, in a pair of navy blue cotton pajamas. Behind her was a bed. A small box fan was set in the windowsill, blowing the cool, rainy air into the room through the open window. Across from the bed, two chairs were set up facing each other at a table with a pot of tea on it, and a cup.

"Hello," she said. I looked at her closely. She looked vaguely familiar. She also looked perfectly calm and unsurprised to see me. It made no sense, and I struggled to reach for the regular, conversational words that had been banished from my brain by adrenaline.

"Yes," I said. "Hi. Are you Rosalind? I'm sorry for coming up here like this. The door was open and I thought I heard someone up here."

"I am. You must be Nancy. Are you looking for your mom?" she asked.

"Yes," I said. "Is she here?"

"She's gone. She's been coming and going, and I'm not sure when she'll be back. She's been working a lot, staying late to do paperwork."

"Oh, okay." Why did it seem as though she felt this exchange was perfectly normal? Her serenity was unnerving. She should have been yelling.

"Would you like some tea? I was just watching a movie, but I was about to switch it off anyway."

"No, thanks," I said. She gestured to me to sit down in one of the chairs, and I did, not knowing what else to do and needing to collect myself. She sat across from me and took a sip from the cup on the table.

There was a black-and-white TV on a low table against the far wall. The image on the screen was of a person sitting on a couch as though mid-interview. The person was saying something in their own defence. Rosalind got up and turned the TV off, and then sat back down.

"I'm happy to have company to distract me from that documentary," Rosalind said. "It came on while I was watching the news channel. I wanted to turn it off, but I couldn't believe what I was seeing. It was an exposé about a fake alcohol treatment centre. There was an Alcoholics Anonymous sign on the lawn of the centre, but it turned out to just be this man's private house. A scam."

"That's so awful," I said. I wanted to ask her about my mom, but I saw that Rosalind looked upset, almost distraught.

"It really is. I don't know how people can do things like that to each other. The guys running the scam, of course, but the relatives too, who brought their loved ones there. Why would they trust a stranger to care for someone they love just because of a name that claims to be some kind of an authority on people's lives, without any proof? I know your brother drinks—that you all worry about him. I know it isn't easy. But I can't imagine you'd turn him over to strangers."

"That's very true," I said. I looked at my watch, wondering if I could call Glen, get him to come over and meet Rosalind, to help me sort things out, if he was awake. It had been an hour and a half since I'd left him. I wanted him to come meet me here and interrupt this strange conversation. He owed me that help, I thought. I shouldn't have to do this alone— why should he leave the worrying to me?

"Can I use your bathroom, Rosalind?"

"Of course," she said. "It's just down the hall, at the front of the house."

I thanked her and went down the hall to the bathroom. It had a bathtub in it, I noticed, as though the floor had, at least at one point, been set up as an apartment separate from the rest of the house. I sat down on the edge of the tub and turned the water on in the sink beside me. I called Glen's phone. It rang its full twelve rings before going to voice mail. I called again. After eight rings, Glen's voice answered.

"Nancy," he said. "Where are you? I've been looking for you. I have to tell you something." His voice sounded slightly thick but better than I would have expected. I heard a car go by in the background on the wet pavement. He was up and walking, outside, so that was good.

"I have to tell you something too," I said. "Why didn't you answer a minute ago, the first time I called? It's kind of urgent—"

"I'm in the rain and it's loud out here with the cars going by. I have to tell you something. I fell asleep for a bit on the couch, and when I woke up I found an insight just sitting there in my mind. I think it was there before, but I just couldn't bring it into focus. Until I slept and woke up."

"I'm sorry, Glen," I said, suddenly flushed with anger, my hands shaking slightly. "But drunken dream insights aren't the kind of help I need right now. I'm at Rosalind's. You have to come over here."

"Why do you think I'm drunk?" he said. "I'm not. I had one drink, and then I had a nap. I'm still waking up, if I sound out of it. I've had enough of this from Kali, planting seeds of doubt so I seem unreliable."

"Okay, fine, you're sober. I know. Then you have to come over here," I said.

"I'm already here. I'm right outside, walking down her street toward the house. I was coming to join you. I'm telling you, I have to tell you something. I know who Rosalind is."

"I know too," I said. All of a sudden I did know. It had been creeping up through my consciousness and now it was there, clear and obvious. "She's mom's old friend, her co-worker from the library, the one who first discovered spontaneous subjectivity transfer. She had a different name before, but it's her." My subconscious couldn't let Glen know it if I didn't.

"Nancy? Are you okay?" Rosalind was at the bathroom door. I hung up the phone, not wanting her to hear me talking.

"I'm fine, thanks!" I called. "Be out in a sec."

I turned off the water, opened the door, and saw Rosalind walking back to her room. She turned to face me, standing in the hall.

"Rosalind," I said. "Did you ever actually experience spontaneous subjectivity transfer?"

"That's what your dad calls it. Your mom and I understand it in a broader way," she said. "We were the ones who felt it, or I was, anyway, and she understood what I meant."

I heard a bang downstairs, the sound of the front door opening.

"Nancy?" It was Glen.

"Who's that?" Rosalind said.

"It's my brother," I said. I went down the stairs and met Glen on the landing. He was wet, and still wearing his muddy tennis shoes. Rosalind came down the stairs behind me.

"Hi, Glen," Rosalind said. "Are you okay?"

"Hi. Yes, I am. Nice to see you again," said Glen. "Nancy, let's just go home. I came to get you." He started walking down the stairs and I saw that he was drunk, after all. Or at least very tired. I followed him outside onto the porch. Rosalind stood behind us at the door. As I walked down the walkway, I almost thought I heard my mom's voice, and Rosalind's responding, but I didn't want to go back into that house when I hadn't been invited.

Glen and I walked down the street together in the middle of the road under the street lights, like the nights in high school when we'd walk home together from parties, bumping into each other and linking arms—except this time only one of us was drunk. I looked at Glen's face beside me in profile and noticed how tired he looked, how much older he'd gotten, and how parallel and straight our walking paths had become, never crossing. Maybe he wasn't drunk, after all, but just tired—I couldn't really say.

EIDOLON

I WORK FOR A TECH COMPANY THAT RECENTLY LAUNCHED a new iteration of an employee-monitoring software. The software's brand name is Eidolon, a name almost as melodious as that of my boss—Iris Mirabello. One drizzly recent morning, Iris and I boarded a plane together to go to a professional conference in New York, as part of promoting the improved version of Eidolon, our company's most important new product. The plane sat on the runway, and we sat in it, side by side, waiting for takeoff. We were both writers in the company's communications department, and we'd been chosen to go to the conference because we knew how to make Eidolon's functions sound as compelling as its name. I was nervous about spending this time with Iris—interested to see her in this new dimension, but also afraid of what she'd see in me. She was probably twenty years older than me, and since I'd met her I'd sensed that she'd lived her life in chapters, and that the current one had opened only relatively recently. She seemed to know a lot.

Iris had been gazing for some ten minutes out the airplane

window, past the runway and into the rainy airfield. This was the first time we'd been in each other's company outside of the office. The back of her head, with its long, dark auburn curls, partly blocked my view of the grey morning. The relief from the chill and awkwardness that would come with take-off couldn't come soon enough.

I'd attributed Iris's abstractedness that morning to the early hour: she'd picked me up in a cab at 5:30 a.m. and had said only four words to me on the way to the airport: "Julie. Don't be sorry," when I'd apologized for knocking her with my carry-on bag. Her statement had been neither reassurance nor rebuke, but hung in the air, caption-like, before dissolving into the fog as we drove off toward the highway to the airport. "Easy for you to say," I'd thought, linking her statement to Iris's defining trait—the policy of never apologizing, never explaining, and never having any cause to.

But now, as she stared silently out the window, turned to face away from me, her hair a kempt mantle, cape-like, on her shoulders and down her back, I thought maybe I was seeing a new side of Iris, and not just literally.

On our way to the airport, we drove past the shiny black building where we worked together, and I thought about how much my life had changed since I was first buzzed up into its noiseless, carpeted interior. I'd started working for a different boss before I worked for Iris, in a cubicle down the hall from Iris's office. I'd first met her in an idea-generating meeting about the company's mission statement. She was the director of communications and a manager of other technical writers. I was included in the meeting as an admin, to take minutes. It was the first time I'd been in the large conference room on the building's top floor with its tall windows and rectangular ship of a table in the centre of the room.

Iris was the first person I saw when I walked into the conference room; she sat like a backward-facing masthead at the prow of the table, even though it turned out she was a participant rather than the leader. The meeting's facilitator, surely no more than half Iris's age, stood behind her at a white board, writing down words; soon, Iris's words were circled and underlined as everyone returned to them, agreeing on their quality. As the meeting's business wrapped up, Iris began to speak off the cuff. She talked about why she'd joined the company. Iris's background, she explained, was in finance—she'd come from another company where she was a CFO, a position she loved. But her respect for the power of words had led her to pursue the writing side of business.

She ended the session with a broad comment outlining a new way forward for our company—a new vision for the role we could play. "We're the leaders, ladies," she said, as she closed out the meeting. "The improved version." I wrote this in the minutes and then deleted it, assuming it was meant for our ears only.

Afterward, I stood in the kitchen of my floor with a co-worker who had also been at the meeting, talking about Iris. This co-worker had started at the company shortly before I had. "She's great with words, but she seems a bit lonely to me," this co-worker said. "You never see her just chatting with other people, relaxing; she's always working when she talks. Once I heard her refer to her team as 'knowledge brokers.' I've never heard anyone talk like her before."

That comment seemed slightly unfair to me, a jab framed as sympathy. Intense professionalism in a woman invites the most intense form of physical scrutiny, a search for the break in the performance; not without unease, I had felt my own eyes begin to watch Iris too closely. Her jackets were linen or silk, her scarves bronze, muted silver, or cream, her pants tailored. Her hair flowed without movement. She answered the demand for beauty with an intelligent radiance whose understatement shone like an honest but appealing answer to a question no one else could face without years of practice. There were rumours about her, and about why she had left her last job, but it was hard to remember or think of these when she was talking.

When I applied for a job under Iris, she seemed willing to take a chance on me. Since then, I've worked as a technical writer under her supervision. The interview for the job went well; I mentioned my dictionaries in an answer to one of the first questions, and I could see that Iris was impressed. As a professional writer, I keep not just an electronic, but also a hard copy, of the *Oxford English Dictionary* on hand wherever I work. The many old leather volumes of it that were the one thing I'd inherited from my grandfather line my office wall, in any office I work in, in any job I hold. The volumes not only help me in my work; they're also my own personal employment insurance. I'd had the books appraised—if I were ever to fall on hard times, selling them would help.

Bringing up the dictionaries at the interview had also taken time away from questions I didn't want to be asked about certain credentials I'd listed on my resumé. I had hoped these details—dates, schools, company names—would have an impressionistic effect, blurring rather than focusing readers' eyes: I had genuinely started the degree the resumé listed, but hadn't finished it; "communications specialist" was also a misleading title for some of the work I'd done in the past.

Truth be told, in my thirtieth year, I'd hit a wall; my marriage ended and I returned to a previous job I'd had at a company that specialized in offering debt consolidation advising services over the phone, before my manager told me I didn't have a knack for making people trust me. "It's like you're here, but you're not," he'd said. I left that job and got a job at a third-party market research company, where I called businesses and covertly gauged and cultivated opportunities to sell them software packages that our company knew were overpriced and ineffective. I still live with the knowledge that I was part of something wrong. The best I can say is that at least I was a bad salesperson. I wasn't a gifted talker. No one—at least not many—had ever actually decided to consolidate their loan or buy a product because of me; but more people could have, if I'd caught them off guard, or had been communicating in writing instead of over the phone.

In my new position, I was so overwhelmed by Iris's choice to give me a break that I didn't have time to think about what I was helping to sell; I focused on the words, on the sound of the name Eidolon, and not what the software would be used for. The technology changes so quickly, people often said around the office; this software we're writing about will be obsolete in a year anyway. Employee-monitoring tools mushroom, meld, and grow subtler, more transparent: from GPS systems and electronic timers locked onto vehicles that make workers streamline routes and jog through errands; to innocuous cameras in the corners of company rooms that offer neutral comments on productivity; to software—like Eidolon—installable on computers, and that can count WPM, read email, see what keys are pressed, and look at all the employee looks at, storing glances, doubts, desperate search terms, and the theft of time. I picture the manuals and book-lets I write turning to ribbons in the shredder when I take breaks from working on fitting words together.

But when I'm inside the words, I don't think, except about the words. I look up the origins and meanings of all new words I learn, including names: it's become my trademark in the workplace as well as in my personal life. Iris's name, whose etymology I've researched, means "Goddess-messenger" and then joins the Latin roots for *wondrous* (*mira*) and *beautiful* (*bellus*) into a single word, her last name. Her parents had been generous.

And Iris had been generous to me. After three months on the job, she invited me to the conference in New York, our chance to make a real name for the improved Eidolon. "Away is the only place to decompress," she said. "Let's go there."

After those ten minutes of Iris's window-gazing, during which I'd gradually succumbed to regular glances at her hair, she turned to me. Had she known that I would be facing her? She met my gaze dead-on, with the same certitude with which she'd claimed the window seat for herself, and answered questions about firearms and hotel addresses at customs. Her face had disappeared—that is, the face I had long strained to peer through to see the face that I thought certainly must lie beneath.

But the face beneath, as I'd imagined it, one flocked with marks of private sadness and fear, was nowhere to be seen. Below her professional face was an identical face, but one without dissembling, without smiling, without that certain angling to the side—that angle some women learn to adjust their heads to instantly when their picture is taken—that she adopted any time you looked at her, the small token of a living portrait of herself, a profile to be tucked in the mind like a business card.

But now, she turned to look at me straight on. She sighed.

"I feel generations-old. Like I've seen the risings and settings of eras," she said.

Before I could ask her what she meant, we were interrupted by the flight attendant asking us to fasten our seat belts. The plane rattled up through the clouds into the part of the sky where only nighttime could stop the sun from shining. When the flight attendant came by again, in the warmth of the yellow light that flooded the plane's cabin, Iris ordered glasses of white wine for both of us, despite the early hour. When they came, they looked like glasses of light.

However odd the trip was proving to be, it was good to get away from my routine. I keep what I think of as a copy of my own mind at work, a section of my mental self reserved for use, at that time, only for the creation of the Eidolon communications. I was happy to leave that copy of me behind, along with the work of creating Eidolon's image in written words. Yet the work was so focused that part of my mind had become stuck in a kind of middle dimension made only of words.

Sometimes, when I needed kindling for the dry work of conveying the procedures for the deployment and use of the Eidolon system, I would look the word *eidolon* up in the dictionary to refresh my sense of it.

The meaning of the word that the software's name plays on is *ghost* or *phantom*. This name was chosen in a competitive spirit, since the most successful analogue of our product currently on the market, the leader among such software, is called Spectre. Their name is better than ours in some ways;

the sound of their word connotes not only *ghost*, to suggest an unseen presence (the monitoring software), but also derives from the Latin for *to look*; so it sounds like familiar words such as *spectator* or *spectacles* that imply the act of seeing. But Eidolon sounds less harsh; it's more mellifluous. And Iris had pointed out that it sounds more refined, less crass. And although it might not be as clearly connected to looking as the word *spectre* is, the word *eidolon* does come from the Greek for *I see*.

What is the experiential difference, the poetic difference, between the meanings of the phrases *to look* and *I see*? I ask this of myself when I'm trying to capture how our product is different from, and superior to, Spectre.

The word *eidolon* can also refer to an idealized person or thing. For example, the dictionary told me through its sample sentence, Petrarchan poetry makes the love object into an eidolon rather than a real person.

Once when I was in a marketing meeting chaired by Iris, I mentioned this other meaning of eidolon; I even brought up Petrarch and courtly love. "I wonder if we could do anything with that," Iris said.

I tried to recall any lines I could dredge up from when I'd studied Petrarch in a university class. I remembered that his poetry was all about paradox, burning and freezing at the same time, love imagined as both prison and freedom. When I got home that night, I looked up and found some lines:

Love kills me not, nor breaks the chains I wear,
Nor wants me living, nor will grant me ease.

I have no tongue, and shout; eyeless, I see;
I long to perish, and I beg for aid;
I love another, and myself I hate.

I made a note of the lines but didn't see what we could do
with the context of love, aside from deepening my brain's relationship with the name of the product I needed to explain
to our customers, which had some value, as I sought to think
of the word and the product in all its facets at once. For a
second, as I stared at the lines on my desk at home with tired
eyes, my brain came unstuck from my work and drifted to
Iris, and why I cared about her so much even though I knew
we could never really get to know each other.

Iris's torpor on the plane was contagious, and was reinforced
by the hum of the recycled air. By the time we landed in New
York, we moved like a unit, circling through customs, pulling our shoes off together automatically, putting them in the
same plastic box, watching them slide together down the belt
through rubber flaps into the X-ray box. We collected our
bags when they went past us on the belt on the other side.

Out on the sidewalk, Iris flagged a cab and we went to the
hotel where the conference was being held. The hotel lobby
was full of milling name-tagged people who looked like they
wanted to be holding drinks. The many eyes of groups of
men reflected Iris as we walked by. "Our event is on the terrace," Iris said. We climbed onto an escalator that took us in
tall zigzags through the hollow centre of the building, past
stands of potted plants and trees that had been growing since
at least the 1980s. On the top floor, Iris took my arm and led
me through a set of glass French doors onto the roof.

Under a large black fabric tent, people in suits stood in

small groups drinking and talking, clustered around heat lamps that made the cold evening feel balmy. A banner stood in one corner, on a pedestal: "Rich Text VIII Welcomes You," it said in gold lettering. "I guess this is the eighth annual conference," Iris had explained. "But it's my first time. It's still a new world for me."

We drifted slowly through the crowd, through the tented warmth, and out the other side. We stopped at the ledge on the edge of the roof. I looked down onto the street, at the cabs pulling up to the door of the hotel and pulling away, far below.

"Look straight ahead, in front of you," Iris said.

I looked straight ahead into and beyond the clouds at the base of the sky, through the cobalt and silver glint of the tall buildings, where a galaxy-shaped whorl of orange, fuchsia, and lavender bloomed.

I turned to Iris on the roof, and away from the sight of the sun setting on the edge of the city. I pulled my thin jacket around me.

"Sunset," I said, not knowing what else to say, overwhelmed by the sound of many conversations around us.

"Yes." She turned to me. She grabbed drinks for us from a tray passing by with glasses of white wine on it. "Here," she said. "A toast, maybe? I've been meaning to tell you something, anyway. That is, I'd like to see both of us freed, to think fully creative thoughts. I really have appreciated the chance—"

"Iris?" A voice from behind us cut Iris off.

Iris turned. A tall, tired-looking woman in black stared at her face like she'd seen a ghost. The woman held a glass of clear liquid that smelled like gin.

"Tonya," Iris said. "Hi. How are you? It's been a while,

hasn't it? We were just talking about going in, but tell me how you are. Julie, this is Tonya, a former colleague. Tonya, this is Julie."

I wondered why Iris didn't introduce me as a colleague, or as her employee.

"What are you doing here?" Tonya asked. I was stunned by the directness of her tone, and by her unwavering gaze.

"Why wouldn't I be here?" Iris said.

"I thought you'd been away," Tonya said.

"You can't keep a good woman down," Iris said, with a laugh.

"No, I guess not."

"Tonya, I see you have a drink. We need a drink ourselves. That's what people do at these things, right?"

"Those who know," Tonya said. She turned to me. "Iris was my boss in another lifetime. Is she yours?"

"Yes," I said.

"I don't think of it that way," Iris said, "as boss and employee, one over the other. Work is shared. We're all together."

"Maybe for you two, but not for me," said Tonya.

"Well, we're at the top together now whether we like it or not, literally," Iris said, with a short laugh, gesturing out toward the view of the city. "There's no getting out of that."

"I'm not here, though. Just my body is. My soul's down there, running down the sidewalk."

Iris laughed. "Did I mention Tonya likes words? We always had that in common. Let's go to our rooms, Julie. It's cold. We can mingle in the morning. Have a good night, Tonya."

"It was nice to meet you, Tonya," I said. Iris turned to go. Tonya looked at me and raised an eyebrow.

Iris took my arm and led me back through the crowd, but

bypassed the escalator, heading into the stairwell. We circled down one floor, then another. "Tonya's a direct person," Iris said, her voice echoing. "We knew each other at a complicated time. Being close to colleagues makes things better but sometimes it can be hard." A tattered white streamer lay on the concrete floor at one landing of the stairs, the last remnant of someone else's party; Iris kicked at it with the toe of her shoe, so that it fell into the space in the middle of the stairwell, straight down the centre of the identical, descending rings of stairs, and disappeared. She opened the door at the seventh floor.

Iris pulled out a key card and opened her room, 716. A large painting over the bed showed a winter field stretching into a white sky, with one thin grey tree on the periphery, so faint it looked translucent. It reminded me of the pendant that hung at the end of a chain around Iris's neck. I'd been staring at it on the plane. It looked like a tree branch or a gold antler.

"I'll go with you to your room and make sure you have everything you need. But first, I need to rest. Sit down," she said, gesturing toward a chair next to the head of the bed. I sat. To my surprise, she threw herself roughly on the bed, face down, diving into it, her arms above her head, her face buried in the pillow. She sighed. Her hair covered her back again, and I couldn't see anything of her face.

"It's good to get away," she said. She turned her head to look at me with one eye. She looked worried. "I can see some of your question marks, Julie: the ones you see around my head, and the ones I see floating around yours."

"Who is Tonya?" I asked.

"She's part of the past. I have a policy of keeping the past taped shut. I know you worry about your past too. I've looked you up. It's not exactly easy to hide these days. We're all rewriting our stories on tracing paper; you can see right through it to the old version."

"I'm not sure about that. I'm feeling confused, actually. How do you know Tonya?" I willed myself to get up and just end the conversation, but I couldn't. I wanted to know who Tonya was, and who Iris was.

"A lot less than she thinks she does. Anyway, I thought we had a deal," she said. "An unspoken one. We don't talk about my past if we don't talk about yours. That's what you hoped for, right? That I would take you as you are, no questions asked? Now, we're here to relax. Turn on the TV. Please. Put on a movie. Let's listen to it with our eyes closed."

I found the remote control in the drawer of the bedside table next to the Bible, and turned on the massive TV with an electronic sound that echoed like a droplet falling from the tip of a stalactite high above us. I flicked through the channels.

"Slower," Iris said. "So that I can hear the voices." I slowed the speed of my channel-changing. "This one," she said. "Stop. Let's listen. Here, this half of the bed is yours. She moved a bit further to the edge of the side she was on. Carefully, I sat down, propping myself among the pillows, my legs hanging off the edge of the bed.

"Are your eyes closed?" she asked.

"Yes," I said. But I kept them open.

I can't believe I sat there and watched that movie beside Iris on her bed, but I did. The movie, called *The Inheritance*, was a psychological thriller, and I let the mechanics of suspense play on the surface of my brain as my other thoughts whirred like background programs. The story was set in San Francisco, about a young woman who works at an investment firm, and her mentor at the company. The protege grows attached to the mentor, who promises her advancement in the company and also offers her friendship and eventually a place to live. In the end, the mentor is led off in handcuffs, as the protege watches from the window, thinking in a voice-over about how they could have arrested anyone at the company but had somehow just chosen one person, her person.

I glanced at Iris ten minutes into the movie, and saw that she was asleep. In her sleep, Iris looked worried. When the movie was over, I checked the TV's guide screen and saw that it had been based on a true story, but that names and details of certain characters had been changed. I resented the way the characters and meanings had been reduced, and wondered how the story had really happened.

I let myself out of her room and padded along the thick white carpet toward my own room. It occurred to me as I stood in front of the door to my room that I could make a run for it, down the stairs or to the escalator, and go out into the night, anywhere, into the second-biggest city in the world; it also occurred to me that I could go back to Iris's room and wake her up and ask to talk about what had happened on the trip. Instead I let myself into my own room and sank into the bed, already almost asleep.

When I'd left my old life, my marriage, my immoral jobs, I just walked away. Walking away in itself felt like an admission that none of it had been real, that who I'd seemed to be and could no longer be had been an imposter. But none of that life had been fake; it had just ended. I was still looking for something to replace it.

THE THIRD PERSON

My FORMER ROOMMATE AND FRIEND ONCE WARNED me that it's never a good idea to socialize with neighbours who live in the same apartment building as you, because if something goes wrong you're stuck with the situation. While I found her warning unnecessarily cautious, I'd nonetheless never made a habit of turning to my neighbours for friendship in the apartment buildings I've lived in. But I've since learned that neighbours can offer an inviting kind of readily available company, especially if they're lonely too. That's how I ended up spending time this past fall with my neighbour, a lawyer named Jolene. Jolene made a good salary, but despite her job, for reasons she revealed to me, her housing budget was similar to my own.

Since quitting grad school a year previously, with the plan of starting my own business selling fabric, and since the plans for the fabric business had been put on hold, I'd been working at the university for two professors in the history department who were co-authoring a biographical monograph. Essentially, I was a transcriptionist, paid to work part-time typing the content of the handwritten letters of the biography's subject, working from digital photos of the letters that my brother Mark had taken when he'd held the job before me.

I'd inherited the transcriptionist position from Mark when he had finished his own degree and got a job as a professor at a university in Oregon. He had recommended me to the professors as a replacement; I'd studied history in the same department, and I typed even faster than him.

I missed Mark and couldn't afford to go visit him, so doing his job felt like a way of keeping in touch. He and one of my closest friends—my roommate, actually; the one who had warned me about socializing with neighbours—had gotten married shortly before they moved away, and it had been hard to find times to talk to either of them on the phone since then; I was finding it more and more difficult to picture them in their daily lives, and I peered after the image of them in my mind with what felt like dimming eyes.

The apartment I rented next door to Jolene's was on the second storey of a two-storey building above a row of three street-level storefronts; the storefront below Jolene's apartment was occupied by the office she worked out of. It was there in her law office that I first met her, just before I moved in; my landlord had asked me to meet with them both there to review and sign my new lease. After she'd taken the landlord and me through the lease, item by item, and the lawyer had left, Jolene and I chatted in her office, and she suggested that we have dinner sometime. "I live just up there," she said, pointing at the ceiling's fluorescent lights. When she looked up to the ceiling, I saw that she had a constellation of faint freckles along her jawline that reminded me of my brother Mark's crooked row of distinct freckles on his cheek, the origin of his nickname: Beauty Mark. I guessed Jolene was in her early to mid-fifties.

"By the way," she asked, as she walked me out onto the sidewalk. "What kind of project are you working on at the university?" I'd listed "Project Manager" on the lease as my profession, instead of "Transcriptionist."

Standing on the sidewalk, I told Jolene about my bosses, and about the monograph they were writing. The monograph was on Sarah Manning, a fairly obscure nineteenth-century American diarist, unpublished novelist, and friend to famous Romantics. I explained that her letters described her descent into a complex spiral of debt that the professors were arguing shed light on the lives of some of the important American Romantics.

"Interesting. Do you enjoy that work?" she asked.

"I'm a fast typist, so it's easy," I said. "And I learn a lot about the period, and about Sarah Manning. That is, when I can read her writing."

It wasn't so much my typing as it was my ability to read Sarah Manning's handwriting that had made me valuable to the professors writing the biography. I'd trained myself to glance across dips, lines, dots, and whirls to catch Manning's intended meanings that often glowed out from behind the lines as much as from the lines themselves. It felt like a relationship I'd built with Manning herself, based on compromise and effort, that afforded me special access to her: the professors had focused in recent years not on the photographs of the letters that I was working from, but on the transcribed documents I'd been giving them. Only Mark, who had photographed the original letters in a museum in a small town in New England, had a closer connection to Manning than I did.

"It doesn't sound easy, working with letters that old. Is her writing hard to read?" Jolene asked.

I found myself telling Jolene about the legibility problem in detail. I had hit a roadblock in deciphering Manning's writing—not in interpreting the meaning of the words, which wasn't my aim, but the decoding of the shape of them, the physical letters and words on the page. In my progress through her papers, I'd come to a slightly frenzied series of letters about money, which were mostly proposals to friends about funds she wanted them to lend her, and her plans to pay the money back when she sold her novel. One of the letters, which the professors had asked me to prioritize, was part of a series that Manning had written to her sister immediately before, on, and just after the date of the death of a man who had been a source of both patronage and pain for Manning. She referred to and addressed this man as "Suzerain," an old word for a feudal overlord. She used archaic language when writing to her sister, seemingly almost as a kind of code, a fact that made the job of deciphering them even harder. The professors expected that this letter would be especially revealing about her life, maybe even a kind of climax in her personal narrative as told by her papers. I had deciphered most of the letter, but there was a whole paragraph of it that was proving stubbornly hard to read, even for me, to whom Manning's handwriting had become as familiar as a voice heard daily.

The problem, as I found myself telling Jolene on the sidewalk, came down to a single perplexing sentence, which I had memorized despite its unclearness. This sentence appeared to read: "My planet's orbit is now not only quick but has also become in its travel cross blast, hurtling not warmly abound but in its cracked way headed straight for the fine of its century star."

"I wish I could help. I don't think I can but I know who might be able to. Bring the letter with you when you come for dinner," Jolene said. "Russel has sharp eyes. He's a writer himself. He can have a look at it. He hasn't had an easy year and I know it would make him feel good to help out."

I wasn't sure who Russel was, but I felt like I'd talked too much already.

"How does this Friday sound?" she asked.

I told her that would be fine and she asked me to come by at seven.

"Russel will also be happy to meet you," she said. "He loves literature, and history. Be sure to bring the letter you were telling me about. He loves a puzzle."

When I arrived at Jolene's apartment, it was she alone who opened the door, and there was no Russel in sight. In fact, it was hard to see much of anything in there, coming in from the still-bright September evening. The apartment's living room, the mirror opposite of my own, was dimly lit. The sole lamp sat on an old rolltop desk that looked recently worked at, strewn with papers, pens, and a calculator. The only other light came from candles, which were placed on a coffee table, a side table, and a dining table. To my surprise, the air inside smelled like stale cigarette smoke.

"Have a seat," Jolene said. We sat on opposite ends of a long, low couch. The room was decorated with what looked like second-hand furniture in an ungainly mix of colours and styles. There was a wooden knick-knack shelf mounted on one wall, with six compartments, three above and three below, and I was distracted by the thought that the shelf could serve as the base of a diorama of our building, with its three units per storey and two storeys.

"Russel apologizes for his lateness today," Jolene said. "He's been sleeping off a migraine this afternoon. He'll come out when he feels human again. In the meantime, it's Friday. That calls for a glass of wine, I think."

An open bottle sat on the table beside three glasses. Two of the glasses had smudges of red residue in the bases. She poured me some into the clean one, and filled one of the others for herself.

"I hope you like red?" she said.

"Oh, of course."

"This is our wine. We make it. Cheaper that way, especially if you go through as much as we do."

The wine was good, although it didn't really taste like wine; it tasted like jam thinned with a mixture of water and wine. After three sips I could feel the muscles in my legs and arms start to relax.

"You're probably wondering why I live this way if I'm a lawyer," she said. "Don't worry, everyone asks."

I hadn't planned to ask but I had been wondering.

"I have some family I'm helping out. Plus some personal debts. Russel works freelance—writing, editing, consulting—and contributes what he can, but it hasn't been easy. We make ends meet. We love to cook. In fact, dinner is all ready, and I think you and I should just go ahead and eat. I don't have much hope for Russel's appetite today."

The dinner consisted of whitefish cooked with butter, herbs and wine, rice, and a green salad with herbs and watercress from pots on the windowsill. As we ate, Jolene asked me questions and I told her things: about my frustrated plans to make a business out of my fabric collection, about my brother Mark and my roommate's marriage and move, and about how I couldn't afford to visit them, and had a nagging feeling I might never see them again. She wove some vague outlines of her own story into the conversation, but it was oddly blank and I didn't feel like I learned much about her. It may have been the wine, or her intent listening, but I shared details with her that I'd never spoken aloud.

After dinner, Jolene opened another bottle of wine and we moved back to the couch.

"I don't want to impose my readings on you already," said Jolene. "But I get the feeling you're someone who cares about people. So I'm going to take a risk and tell you something about myself. A problem I'm having. I'm hoping that when Russel gets up he can help you by looking at the letter. I always like to give something in return if I ask for something, so I promise I'll get him up if he's not with us in a half-hour, but in the meantime, do you mind if I share something with you?"

"No, of course not," I said. I couldn't help but feel distracted, unfocused, not only because of the third large glass of wine I'd started on, but because of her repeated mentions of the Manning letter, along with the seemingly imminent appearance of a third person in the room. I couldn't help but wonder why she didn't offer to look at the letter herself—since she seemed so interested in it, and because she was a lawyer, and I therefore assumed she was experienced in looking at documents in detail. I wondered what made her so confident in Russel's abilities as an exceptional reader. In any case, I hoped I would be able to respond adequately to whatever she was about to say.

"There's no way of saying this that doesn't sound dramatic,"

Jolene said. "The reality is that Russel is in a bad way right now. The migraine is just one of the symptoms of what he's going through—he's weaning himself off the pills he takes for his insomnia and anxiety. I won't tell you the name of the pills. I don't want you to be tempted to look up the withdrawal symptoms that come with quitting and the nine hundred side effects, everything from tooth pain to hallucinations. God, it's awful what they'll prescribe, for years, without asking any questions. But the pills are just a secondary problem. He got started on them in the first place because he can't sleep. The reason he can't sleep is our money trouble. Basically, to speak plainly, we've been the victims of identity theft. Russel has, and I've had to pay and pay to bail him out. It's ruined everything."

I looked at her, hoping she would give me more anchoring information before I'd have to respond.

"Last year, Russel tried to move out into his own apartment, but when the landlord checked his credit he was refused. And then he started getting calls from collection agencies about overdue balances on credit cards from banks neither of us had ever even heard of. I was glad he ended up staying here with me, but I also want better for him than this life framed by debt."

At that moment, I heard a bumping sound from the direction of the dark hallway.

"Hi," a low voice said. "You must be Lois. Hi. I'm sorry I missed dinner."

Jolene threw me a glance that said our conversation about Russel was over. "Russel!" she said. "Hi!"

A man about a year younger than me came into the room. He wore a rumpled T-shirt and a pair of black track pants. He had dark circles under his eyes. His hair was so short it must have been freshly shaved within the last few days. He looked exhausted.

"Russel. Can I get you something to eat?"

"No, thanks," he said. He reached for the bottle of wine on the table and filled a glass. He pulled a pack of cigarettes out of his pocket and lit one. At first I saw it as a sign of indulgent tolerance that Jolene didn't tell him to go outside to smoke, but then he held the pack out to her and she took and lit one for herself.

"Are you sure you want to drink, Russel?" Jolene asked.

"I'm very sure," he said to Jolene. He looked at me. "My mom worries about me too much."

"Oh, you're mother and son," I said, barely able to conceal my surprise. I'd expected a husband.

"Did you think she was my live-in lawyer?" he asked me, laughing. His eyes looked sleepy.

"Oh, no. I just wasn't sure."

"My brilliant and cheeky son, Russel. Russel, I was just telling Lois about how much you read," Jolene said. "How you can read anything."

"You must be really impressed," he said to me, laughing. "My mom thinks it's not bragging if it's about me, rather than herself."

"Russel. Actually, Lois is impressed, and interested. Lois has a letter she's hoping you'll have a look at. A historical document. Lois, do you have the letter?"

I went to my purse, where the printout of the photograph of the original Manning letter was folded. I laid it on the coffee table and smoothed out the creases. I explained to Russel who Manning was, and told him about the previously unexamined papers I was transcribing, and their significance to the history of the period.

"Jolene tells me you're a good reader," I said to Russel. "This is the sentence I'm having trouble with. Here." I pointed at the line in question.

Russel pulled a candle toward him across the table, and held the letter up in front of it, so that the light shone through the paper from behind it.

"'My planet's orbit is now not only quick but has also become in its travel cross biast, hurtling not warmly about but in its crooked way headed straight for the fire of its centring star,'" Russel said.

"'Cross biast'?" I said. "Are you sure? Not 'blast'?"

"No, it's definitely 'biast.' It's a metaphor from the game of bowls. A ball in motion was 'cross-biased' when it was knocked off its straight course by another ball. She's comparing her planet to a ball that's been knocked off its course by another ball—knocked out of its regular orbit around the star that kept it warm. It's now headed straight for that star, to be burnt up by its heat."

How did he know so much about this topic? If he was an expert in my bosses' field and Jolene hadn't thought this fact worthy of mention to me, then—what? Then, maybe anybody could do what I did, and do it better. I became aware that I felt threatened by his casual expertise. I was at a loss for words, but needed to respond.

"You're definitely a good reader. An amazing reader. How did you learn to read like this?"

He shrugged with one shoulder. "I have an interest in forensic handwriting analysis. I'm self-educated and it's one of the areas I've focused on. One of the benefits of opting out of formal school is that you can learn how to do things that no one else knows how to do."

"Well, you're indispensable to me right now," I said. "I was about ready to give up and quit."

"Quitting is usually a bad idea," he said. "But it can be fun, if you have the means and opportunity. Speaking of which, I think I'm going to have to go back to bed. I wanted to at least say hi, but it's been one of those days. I hope you'll come again when I can stay up." Russel stood up and retreated to bed, leaving Jolene and me alone in the room.

Jolene went to pour me another glass of wine, but as politely as I could I covered the top of my glass with my hand.

"Well, then, I hope you won't mind if I have just one more half-glass on my own. It's been good talking to you tonight. There are some things that are better kept between two people," said Jolene. "But sometimes only an outside perspective can break open a bad pattern. I don't keep secrets from my Russel. But I do try to protect him from isolation. And I think maybe you can help. You can be a friend to him, I think; the kind of friend I can't be. Do you think it would be okay if he visits you once in a while? You said yourself at dinner that you miss your brother. Maybe Russel could be company for you too."

If I'd known that the price for the letter's translation would be accepting a stand-in version of Mark, I would have thought twice about accepting the insight. Jolene was looking at me too closely, like we were coming to an agreement. I thanked her for the dinner and said I had to go because I was feeling tired. I went downstairs, out onto the street, where the cool air soothed my hot forehead and spinning head. Upstairs in my own apartment I fell into bed and was asleep within minutes.

The next morning, I typed out an email to the professors, explaining what I'd learned, and telling them about the sentence. When I checked my email fifteen minutes later, they had both already responded, commending me and saying how thrilled they were.

I'd already known why the information Russel had given me about the planet metaphor was important: the planned subtitle of Manning's unpublished novel was "The Crooked Orbit." I'd discovered that information in one of her earlier letters. The sentence in the letter was clearly a verbal link to the unfinished novel, shedding new light on the context. As I interpreted it, the central man depicted in her novel was a fictional version of Manning's personal patron, the man her letters show was more to her than simply a patron.

I sat on my bed, pressing my temple to stop the pulse of pain that moved up and down the side of my head. I pictured a planet circling its star, and then being knocked out of its orbit by an errant planet or asteroid hurtling out of nowhere from space. How had Manning known so much about astronomy?

My doorbell rang. I pulled on some clothes, and went downstairs and opened the door. It was Russel.

"Hi," he said.

"Hi," I said.

"I came to say sorry for the state I was in last night. I hope I didn't ruin your night. I know it can be strange moving into a new building, not knowing anyone, and we do want you to feel welcome."

"Thanks," I said. I didn't know what else to say yet.

"Have you had coffee yet?" he asked.

"Can you come in for a coffee?" I asked. I needed to sit down and didn't want to stand in the door talking.

Upstairs, he sat on the futon that served as my couch. I dumped some ground coffee and water into my coffee maker and it started dripping. I sat down across the room from him on a footstool by the door and left the door open.

"My bosses are thrilled about the letter," I said. "The sentence you figured out."

He shrugged. "It's not like I have that much else going on. Happy to help."

"Your mom said you work freelance. You should let me know what I owe you for your services."

"No, of course not," Russel said. "It was no trouble."

"But without you I would have been stuck," I said. "I'd like to pay you."

"Don't worry about that. This isn't what I came to talk to you about. I came for another reason, a more important one. That is, I wanted to ask you something. Can I see one of Manning's other letters?"

"Okay," I said. I went to my desk and got the folder of printouts of the digital pictures Mark had taken of the original letters in New England, and handed it to Russel. He opened the folder and leafed through them, starting with the early ones, frowning, and then moving quickly forward to the set of more hurried letters that I'd separated from the pile with a paperclip—the ones the professors had asked me to view as the potential climax of Manning's papers.

Russel set the paperclipped letters aside on the table.

"You're good with Manning's handwriting yourself, right?" he asked.

"Pretty good," I said. "Very good."

"Then you must have wondered the same thing I'm wondering—were these messier letters written by the same person as the other letters? Are they even genuine?"

I paused and chose to let him continue.

"It does say 'cross biast.' I interpreted the sentence like I saw it. I just did what I was asked."

"I think I know what you're saying, but please go on."

"It's hard to describe my process. I'm not sure what you find, but for me, when I transcribe, it's like I hold my mind's breath. I let seeing take over for a second. I know for that moment through my eyes only, like the optic nerve is all I have. You can only do it if you accept the knowledge whole, whatever it is, and take it on its own terms. And what I'm saying is that part of what I saw in those letters is that the lines on that page are young, not old. They were written recently. I don't know how else to put it, but there was too much effort there: in the handwriting, in the words themselves. I felt them trying to be rather than being. I felt that as clearly as I read the words of the sentence."

I paused again. "I don't get it," I said.

"We don't have to go into it. I shouldn't have raised it. I just wondered if you had ever considered the possibility that these letters, or some of them, aren't genuine. That someone might have forged them."

I thought of Mark and his camera. How easy it would have been to slip forgeries in with the other letters and take pictures of them. But that was ridiculous. Why would he change her letters? And how could he think he wouldn't be caught? And besides, he wouldn't do that.

"It's not possible," I said. "I don't want to talk about it. It's stupid." I was aware that I sounded rude, but I needed the line of thought running uninvited between me and this stranger to stop.

"Okay. I think I must just be paranoid—I guess that happens when someone steals your identity. I know my mom told you about that. It's okay. But I'll just say one thing. Keep a close eye on your mail. And keep an open mind when it comes to fraud. It really happens. And when it does, you never have the luxury of being just one person again. My mom and I will never be on our own again. There's always a third, joining us from an invisible dimension. One that doesn't keep us company but won't leave us alone."

He looked like he was going to go on. But I stood up. He did too, and I told him about the work I still had ahead of me for the day. I asked him to thank his mom for the dinner. He said he would, and then he left.

I started getting ready to go to work, setting out the things that I use as anchors at each corner of my desk: mug, waterglass, magnifying glass, cluster of three pens. I planned to work all day on the rest of Manning's letters; they needed to be typed out, and not only because I needed the job—but because the job needed me, Manning needed me, and she and I had a bond now: I'd help her to talk no matter who had written the words she was saying.

ALDEN

LAST SUMMER, I DECIDED TO DROP EVERYTHING AND move to a small town called Alden, which I'd never been to before, to start a new job. It was a one-year contract, so I figured I could leave after the first year if it didn't work out. After all, when I say I dropped everything, there wasn't much to drop—a fact illustrated by the amount of time I spent talking on the phone to my new boss, Grant, in the weeks leading up to my move. Grant seemed to love the phone, and my days were open—almost as open as Alden itself, as Grant described it.

Alden was a former railroad town two hours' drive away from the big city I was living in. "There's one thing we have a wealth of here in Alden," Grant told me several times on the phone, "and that's space. We're rich in space." I'd lie in my undershirt on the floor of my small basement apartment in the hot, August city, talking to Grant about Alden. I would try to picture the space he was describing, the idea of freely moving air, open streets, and empty buildings. During the month-long lead-up to my move, we talked a couple of times a week. It was a lonely time, but also a time of anticipation.

After finishing a master's degree in English, I'd been teaching communications at a college in the city off and on for three years, until a bad experience on campus prompted me to leave.

I'd gotten into the habit of leaving sandwiches on a bench in a concrete courtyard outside the classroom I taught in, because I'd seen a woman through the window leaving the courtyard one morning, and I believed she was sleeping there at night. But then I got a letter from security saying that I'd been reported by a community member for leaving garbage on the campus, and I didn't see the woman again after that. I'd been thinking of leaving the college anyway, and the letter made the time feel right to move on. I knew I should stay to work on the situation, but instead I walked away.

Grant's outside-the-lines thinking struck me as a welcome shift change from what I'd come to see as an unfeeling bureaucracy at the college. And my sister, my closest friend in the city, had recently moved away for a job, so it made all the more sense to look for something else, somewhere else.

Later that summer, after not working for a few months, aside from some freelance editing work, I saw a job posting online for the one-year contract with the city of Alden as their marketing and communications officer, and applied. Grant called me within the same week to tell me they were interested in talking to me. When he said "talking" he meant just that, it turned out. They let me do a phone interview for the job. Grant never even mentioned the possibility of Skype, or of me visiting by train or in a rented car, expenses I'd started calculating as soon as I got his first call. But no such expenses turned out to be necessary. Everything was paid for by his plan—Alden's plan.

"You'll see what I mean about space when you drive in," he explained again, about a week before my move. "Houses, warehouses, offices, schools, stores: we have spaces of all kinds. It may look empty. I don't want to deceive you about what you're getting into. But I hope and expect that we'll look on the space as an opportunity. You'll see what I mean."

Grant's title was Cultural Affairs Officer. He himself had recently been hired by the corporation of the town of Alden. Alden's main landmark had been a large, turn-of-the-century military academy, but it had shut down in the 1970s after a financial scandal. An Alden citizen named Allen Poole had bought the Victorian building, converting it into a music conservatory, and then, when that failed, a retirement community, before it finally fell into disuse, sat vacant for half a decade, and was burned down by arsonists who were never identified. Grant said that part of our job would be brainstorming about new uses for the large academy grounds that now sat empty, aside from the building's foundations

In those final, hot days in the city, lying sweating in my tiny apartment, waiting out the need to eat as long as possible, turning radio programs spoken in languages I didn't know to high volume to block out traffic sounds that poured in through the always-open window, with its screen torn from the box fan I kept in it, I'd appreciated Grant's phone calls as a dispatch from another world altogether. I was entertained by the fact that he only called, and never emailed, and by the strange intimacy of talking to someone so frequently who knew nothing about me.

I did see what Grant meant about space when I arrived in Alden.

It was raining lightly in the mid-sized town north of Alden where I got off the train, and the cab was there waiting for me. ("You're Curtis's guest, right?" Curtis, I'd learned, was Grant's assistant.) Grant had explained that the closest I could get to Alden by train was a half-hour drive away, and from there a cab was the only option. (That was one of the things we could brainstorm about together, Grant had said— the transportation situation.) The driver lifted my two large suitcases into the trunk; I'd brought what I cared to keep, and gotten rid of the rest.

The cab flew in solitude along a small highway, past silos, a distant fenced yard where a horse stood, head lowered, and fields where rows of orange gourds and yellow summer squashes sat in lines on the soil, glowing in the bright grey daylight. The white-haired driver's face in the rear-view mirror was pale and lined; his grip on the wheel and ease with his turns said he'd driven these roads most of his life. A manila envelope—the one communication I'd received from Grant or his office that wasn't a phone call, the one piece of evidence that I had any business coming to town—was getting damp from my sweaty hands. The thought that this whole thing could be a scam had occurred to me, but I'd pushed it out of my mind. A friend of mine had accepted a job at a university abroad teaching music; when he got there, it turned out the university didn't exist, except as a website. There was no job, and money he'd sent at the request of his contact for accommodations and travel expenses had disappeared into thin air. At least I'd sent no money, I thought; if things turned out not to be what they seemed, I'd just turn around and leave.

The envelope's contents had provided welcome, more tangible backup to the story Grant had given me about Alden's situation and his role in it. Mr. Allen Poole, the son of a long-serving mayor, and grandson of one of the military academy's founders, had made a bequest to the town, including cash, as well as several houses and buildings that were to be put to new use by Grant, in keeping with Poole's wishes for Alden's future. Mr. Poole had specifically bequeathed the funds and assets to Grant, and Grant had been hired formally by the city as a director in charge of promoting growth and vitality. One of the properties bequeathed by Allen Poole was the house I'd be staying in—called Founder's House; another was the lot where the ruins of the burned-down academy stood.

"One good thing," Grant had explained, "is that Allen's bequest means we can put you up in style. I think you'll be very comfortable." Alden's plan was to entice new employees there with the offer of free accommodations in unused, city-owned houses. The package in the envelope was the one concrete sign I had that anything he'd said was true. I opened the envelope and checked for the hundredth time that the key to the house I'd be staying in was still there. I pulled out a stapled, photocopied package of information about Alden and looked at it again.

The final page of the stapled package was titled "Founder's House—Orientation," in a cursive font. It explained that the house had been the family home of the Poole family, where Allen Poole had grown up. I was still expecting that there had been some mistake about this detail, that I'd be staying in an apartment in the house, rather than in the whole house. I was staring at a small picture of the house at the bottom of the page, its finer details inscrutable—was that stained glass? I loved stained glass, and had never lived in a building that had any—when my phone rang. My "hello" elicited a glance, with raised eyebrows, in the rear-view mirror from the cab driver, then a nod, and a drop of his eyes back into meditative highway gazing.

"We're so happy you're on your way," said Grant, on the other end. "And I'm so happy you'll be staying in Founder's House. I know what it's like trying to live in the city these days. Everyone fighting over a square foot of land or a one-room basement apartment."

My mind raced, and I flushed—had I told him about my apartment? I thought I had studiously concealed my circumstances ("Freelance, right now" instead of "unemployed," "between opportunities" instead of "recently gave up," "researching new fields" instead of "adjusting expectations"). No, I hadn't said a thing, and certainly nothing about my apartment. He must have been speaking in generic terms.

"Founder's House is one of Alden's gems. We wanted to make things nice for you during your stay. I shouldn't say this, but we got hundreds of applications for your job. But we feel fortunate that it's you we chose."

The cab pulled off the highway, following a sign to Alden, and turned onto a long street that was empty at first except for the odd garage or gas station, and then, as we entered town, became lined with storefronts.

"This is the main drag up here," said the cab driver.

There were real estate signs on almost every building. Before I could take much of it in, we turned right.

"We're headed down toward Founder's House," said the driver. "This used to be the wealthy part of town, down by the lake."

Sailing south down an empty residential street lined with

increasingly bigger houses, we came to the top of a hill, and as we came over it, with a drop in my stomach, I saw the sky dip down ahead of us, to meet a thick line of deeper blue.

Over the hill, the street began sloping steadily downward, toward the water, and the houses became massive, rambling Victorian structures. I ran my finger over the shape of the key through the paper, not knowing quite what to say to the driver, but feeling like I should share my admiration for the sheer size of the houses. I lifted my phone to the window and tried to hold it steady enough to frame a few of them as we passed. Some were so big they were hard to even see in their entirety at once, in their many-sidedness, with multiple storeys, gables, turrets, stacked porches; one red house was so big that it looked like it had a whole second house growing out of the side of it, as though its ethereal self had frozen mid-stride as it stepped out of its body to walk away.

Some of them looked loved. I took a picture of a tire swing hanging from a willow tree, and a calico cat sitting in front of a wheelbarrow full of sticks and leaves with a pair of faded work gloves hanging over one rusted side. But many of them, at least half or even more, looked under-tenanted, empty, or abandoned. Porches sagged, ivy grew up over brick, or even right over windows.

"Vacancy," the cab driver said.

I started, and looked at him in the rear-view mirror. We had paused at a stop sign. I wondered if he was talking to himself, and felt disconcerted. He was staring across the road, and my eyes followed his line of vision. He was shaking his head.

"That's just a shame," he said. "Graffiti everywhere."

The word "Vacancy" was written in massive, spray-painted, mock-elegant cursive letters across the face of a yellow house. The red letters had been scrubbed at until they had turned pink, and the faded colour had an incongruously gentle effect against the white-trimmed, pale-yellow brick, like writing on a cake. The clouds had begun rolling around the sky, opening cracks of faint blue, and as I looked at the decorated house, a ray of early fall sunlight bathed the brick, lighting up the letters. I found it odd that I hadn't seen any people walking around, or on the porches of any of the houses.

"Don't pay much attention to that," the driver was saying. "I've seen it happen in other generations, but the town comes back from it, and then the visitors come back. I used to work for the city myself, driving seniors—before I was a senior myself. Between good times, kids around here get bored. There's not enough to do. It's a lovely old neighbourhood, lots of history. The military academy was just down the way—it was famous. It still is, even though it burned down a while back now. Lots went on here right in this block or so. Politicians used to live here. The mayor. Which brings us to our final stop. To our right, Founder's House." He pulled to a stop in front of the Victorian mansion that I recognized from the picture in the information package, and I got out.

It was the biggest building I'd ever approached as a resident. But the thought of living anywhere so large, the idea of such a large structure housing a space that was private rather than public, unshared, without "open" hours, came over me in a rush of what I can only describe as a combination of fear, disbelief, and more than a little greed.

My phone began to vibrate in my pocket, and I pulled it out. Grant was calling. I sent the call to voice mail, intending to call him once I got inside, not wanting to interrupt the silence of the neighbourhood. A second later, I got a text from him: "The house is all yours. Make yourself at home." Alden seemed willing to speak to me only in disembodied voices:

Grant's voice on the phone, the written word in graffiti on the house. But no, that word wasn't for me. Or maybe it was, and it was telling me what I suspected—that I wasn't supposed to be here. At least not like this, invited not by the town, but by a single voice that might just have been an echo of a single voice, an echo of my own.

A bird landed in a tall tree in the yard of the house across the street behind me, and I thought I could hear its individual feathers sifting the air. I lifted the phone up to my eye and took pictures of the stained-glass windows, each composed of leaf-sized droplets of coloured glass that together formed an image of a lion among eagles and peacocks against a backdrop of gold and green.

I pulled the key from the envelope and unlocked the front door, which led into a foyer with a stained-glass transom above a second, inner door, which stood ajar. I took a picture of the transom on my phone, before going through into a large wood-panelled hallway.

Rooms of panelled wood to all sides of me gleamed in the sunlight they absorbed from small windows. Twin living rooms flanked the front hall, decorated sparsely, with an '80s chair-and-loveseat set in each. I imagined parties of the Poole family and guests moving from room to room, or sitting for family dinners in the dining room, and felt that it couldn't be right for the house to be opened to just one person.

I wondered if I should call Grant, but decided I would look around upstairs first, to find my bearings. Up past a window seat on a landing that looked out over an overgrown side yard, I passed second-floor bedrooms, one furnished with just a large bed, one empty except for a telephone on the floor. At the end of the hall, a third door had a small handwritten sign taped on it: "Theresa's Room."

Sitting on the bed in my room, I stared at a framed print of a painting of willow trees on the wall before I got up to go back downstairs. On my way down, on the wall beside the head of the stairs, I noticed a fourth, thinner door, which looked like it must lead to an attic. There was a sign on it: "Debbie's Room." Maybe I wasn't alone, after all. I knocked on the door, but was answered with silence. I was thirsty, so I went back downstairs, through the dining room and into the kitchen, toward a sink, and started opening cupboards.

A flurry of quick knocks behind me set my heart racing. I grabbed the sink and turned around. Framed momentarily in the kitchen-door window was the face of a man in a shirt and tie. The door opened, and he stepped inside, arm already extended for a handshake.

"Theresa. Welcome. I'm Grant. So good to finally meet you in person. I tried calling but couldn't reach you. I wanted to be here so that there'd be a familiar face to greet you when you arrived."

I guessed he meant "a familiar voice." The face I'd pictured, which had become familiar in my mind, to the point where I'd assumed, unconsciously, that I would probably recognize him when I saw him, wasn't like I'd pictured it at all. He had dark hair in thick waves that looked like they'd been subdued with a gelled comb. Deep circles ringed his eyes. He wore a stiff white shirt and a plain grey tie.

"You must be hungry," he said. "Have you eaten?"

"I'm just a bit thirsty," I said. "But I couldn't seem to find a glass."

"No glasses?" he said. "We'll have to fix that. Do you like apples? Or pears?"

"I like apples," I said. "And pears. I like both."

He held his hand to show me a clear plastic bag of apples and pears.

"I brought you a fruit bowl," he said. "Well, not the bowl, but the contents." He set them down on the counter. "But you want more than fruit after your long trip. Come on. Let's go get you a drink and I'll show you around."

I was feeling already like this had been a mistake, but I was overwhelmed by the house. I wanted to sleep in it just one night, at least, and feel its size and silence all around me, even though the idea of being alone there scared me. But then I recalled the sign saying "Debbie's Room." Maybe I wouldn't be alone after all. I would give it at least the night to see what happened.

Grant's car was parked down the street. The driveway was muddy, he explained. The car was a white Escalade SUV.

"The city's car," he said, as we got in. "One of the perks."

The interior smelled like leather. We started driving down the hill, toward the lake. We passed a set of tennis courts, closed up with big locks and heavy chains, but with a chain-link fence that had been cut open from the bottom, to form a kind of curtained entrance just big enough for one person. There were no nets. Big cracks in the pavement grew thick with ragweed and goldenrod.

"There's something sad about abandoned tennis courts, isn't there?" Grant said. "It seems like such a waste. A tennis court is such a cool thing to do with space."

"It's true," I said, my head feeling light. I wondered why the courts hadn't been resurfaced. Maybe the kids in town would like a place to play tennis, if the town could provide rackets and balls, an instructor, and maybe set up some drop-in hours. But I was so thirsty it was hard to think. The sun had come out now, and it was shining through the window on my side onto my legs, in the still and airless car.

"I'm sorry, but if we could find a drink for me soon, I'd be really grateful," I said. "I haven't had a drink since I left the house."

"They didn't offer you a drink on the train? I guess rail travel really isn't what it used to be. We're going to make that up to you. I'm taking you somewhere special for a welcome-to-Alden toast."

He veered toward a field with stone walls placed at irregular intervals in it. As we got closer, I saw the ruins of a large building in a field—the location of the military academy. One small building remained, a chapel with boarded windows and a spire. There was another small, square building across the field that looked intact, but elsewhere on the grounds, tall, wide piles of stone and brick sat; sections of the ground were tiled, what remained of its bathrooms. Much of the rock was charred. On the spire of the chapel, vertical red lettering had been scrubbed from the white stone, a word that had been painted sideways down the spire's length. Only the faint word "Vacancy" was clearly visible, written left to right at the spire's base.

"This is the academy," he said. "That's the old music building, right ahead. Allen restored it when he tried to turn the place into a conservatory, before the fire. It was the only building that stayed standing, and one of the most beautiful. It's going to be your office." He was pointing toward the one other building, aside from the chapel, that was intact. This one looked relatively unblemished, like it had been restored.

"But I thought my office was going to be at the town hall. I assumed I'd be working from there."

"Our team is going to be right here. We're town employees, but we're almost like independent contractors working with the town, if you look at it from another perspective. I'm officially hired, but I'm also kind of a free agent, because of the way the money flows. Since you work for me, you're an agent of a free agent. You're going to love the building." He turned off the Escalade in front of the music building and we got out. He hadn't answered my question, so I made a mental note to bring up later the matter of why we were located in the ruins rather than at the town hall.

We walked up a flagstone walkway, and Grant opened the door. Stepping inside, I found myself in a thickly walled room with wooden floors that shone like they'd just been refinished. A piano stood in one corner, and instruments of all kinds hung on stands mounted on the walls: violins, cellos, violas. Everything gleamed red-gold. A drum set stood in another corner.

"Mr. Poole was on the chair of the board of directors for the academy. It was his influence that led to the music building getting added to the academy, and music to the curriculum. When we renovated it to use it for our office, we thought we would decorate in a music theme. We had all of Allen's instruments anyway, so we put them in here."

Three massive, mission-style, solid-oak desks were placed against three of the four walls, each turned to face a large, stained-glass window. At one of these desks, a woman sat with her back to us, a long braid running down her back. She turned her head to the side, and I saw a headphone in her ear.

"Oh, hi," she said, pulling the headphones out and standing up to meet us. "Hi, Grant. And you must be Theresa. I'm Debbie. I'm looking forward to working with you. I understand we'll also be living in Founder's House together."

Debbie was tall, over six feet. She wore a tailored red dress and jacket. I felt underdressed.

"Debbie arrived last week," Grant said. He hadn't mentioned that I'd be living and working with someone else, but I wasn't sure why I should be surprised.

"You're my downstairs neighbour at Founder's House," said Debbie. "I'm on the third floor."

"Hi. Nice to meet you," I said. "I saw the door to your room."

"Debbie's just back in town after living away for several years," said Grant. "But Alden is Debbie's hometown. You can't take the Alden out of the girl."

"I went away for school," said Debbie. "I studied music. It's a testament to Grant that he was able to be friendly with Mr. Poole. Not many made it past his guard. My mom worked for him for years and never really got to know him."

"He was always lovely with me," said Grant.

"Allen was like the patriarch of Alden. His grandfather was one of the academy's founders. Hence the name Founder's House," said Debbie. "His name was Allen but many people called him Alden, because he had so much power in town. He was a cellist too; he taught me to play, the one time he really engaged with me or my mom, even though we were almost like a part of the family, because she cleaned for him and I helped her sometimes. I would have stayed here to study if his music conservatory idea had worked. But he left money in his will for me to go away to school, so I'm lucky. I can't exactly say I liked him, but we have a lot to thank him for—including our jobs."

"We are lucky, Debbie," Grant said with a laugh. "We're lucky you're back."

"Thanks," Debbie said, turning back toward the desk and placing her headphones in the drawer.

"We're happy you're reunited with Alden," said Grant. "And Allen, too, in a way, eccentric fella that he was. We'll drink to him, and to us. Now, did I remember to put some champagne in the fridge?"

Deb went to a mini-fridge in a corner and opened the door. "No, but I did," she said, pulling out a bottle, and handing it to Grant.

"Sparkling wine," he said. "This will work." He popped it open and poured wine into plastic cups that Deb took from a package on top of the fridge.

"I think Allen would be happy to know you've joined us," said Grant. "Happy to know our team is going to bring new life to this old town."

"To Allen," Deb said. "And to Theresa."

"To all of us." Grant said.

We drank. I worried about the strangeness of this whole set-up. I was concerned about our office on the grounds of a burned-down academy, and how little I understood about what I would be doing during my contract. I filed the thought that I could leave tomorrow, and turned back, resetting a face that concealed my worry and fear. For a moment I banished all thoughts and enjoyed the pleasure of quenched thirst; I drank a second glass of sparkling wine and started to feel better. After all, Debbie seemed nice enough—maybe I could get the full story and a better understanding of things from her.

"Well, dinnertime seems to be upon us," said Grant. "Shall we head back to the house?"

Debbie and I got out of the car at Founder's House. I assumed we would go in alone, that I would get a chance to ask her some questions over dinner, about how the benefaction from Allen Poole worked exactly, and if she knew Grant's backstory. But Grant got out of the car with us.

"Curtis was going to have dinner set up for us," said Grant.

Curtis hadn't let Grant down. Inside, platters of food had been laid out on the sideboard, covered with draped tea towels. A bottle of red wine sat behind the platters, beside three wide-bowled wineglasses, and a stack of three plates and three sets of cutlery rolled up in fabric napkins.

Grant opened the wine, and Debbie uncovered the food: cold roast beef, cold salmon, a cold vinaigrette potato salad, and a cold green bean salad. We ate and drank, and I felt better. I relaxed and drank my wine. Grant talked about the area's history, about how the unused train tracks made Alden the best place in the world for a fall walk. You could weave sidelong through town, at odd angles that offered internal views unfettered by the auto-correcting guidance of streets. "There's potential there," he said. "I know it. Migratory birds like the throughways of the rail passages, so why can't we get people to migrate there to enjoy Alden?"

Once we'd finished eating, Debbie said, "It's lovely to meet you, Theresa. But I'm beat. It's time for bed for me. Let's have a coffee in the morning and chat some more." We said goodnight to Debbie. I noticed she carried her glass of wine with her.

Debbie's footsteps stopped halfway up the stairs. Her shape blocked the moonlight that fell through the stained-glass window on the landing onto the hall floor below. The broken pieces of light disappeared. She must have been sitting on the window seat on the landing centred against the window.

"Now," Grant said to me, filling our glasses with an inch and a half of wine, as though measuring out the length of time needed for the conversation to follow. "Tomorrow. Your first day. We have big plans. We want to try to start advertising widely in the cities. Why can't Alden be an option for people who can't break into the real-estate market back where you came from, for instance? Young professionals."

"Advertising what?" I said. It came out more rudely than I'd intended. "Not housing, right? I don't really have any real-estate experience."

I heard Debbie get up from the landing and go up the second half of the staircase. A door at the top of the stairs opened and shut.

"I kind of thought this job was about getting some new things going with people who already live here," I continued. "Our phone calls. I thought that's what we were talking about. I wanted to meet the people who live here and hear from them."

Grant looked at me, fixing me with eyes so serious that I thought about jumping up and clearing dishes from the table to the kitchen, to create a distraction. But then he laughed.

"Oh, I think I see," he said. "You thought this was going to be a kind of escape. A fantasy of life in a small town. You as the centre of things in a place where stakes are low for you and high for everyone else."

I stared at him, my heart racing and my face hot. Was he drunk? I couldn't tell. The wine was almost gone: a second bottle he'd taken from the cabinet in the sideboard when we'd finished the first one was almost empty. But his speech wasn't slurred. I was drunk, I knew. The place where we sat felt like a still, lit centre around which the dark surroundings spun.

"I'm going to bed now," I said. "We can talk about plans tomorrow. Mine have most likely changed." I was already starting to plan, to sober myself up, thoughts galloping: I could reassess in the morning, could make plans to go back to the city; I could stay with a friend until I could find a place of my own, maybe a place with a roommate, until I sorted out what I could do. My reservations were clear enough: about living in a house with Debbie, about working for Grant, and about the ideas he had about the job I was going to do; about the fact that it seemed normal to Grant that we had gotten drunk together on my first night in town; about the fact that my office was going to be in a burned-down school. About Grant insulting me. About my idea that any place would be easier than any other.

"Okay. Tomorrow will be good," he said. He got up, stretching. "We'll have a good talk. I'm looking forward to working with you, Theresa." I guessed he either hadn't heard or hadn't understood what I said, that my plans had changed.

When I got upstairs to my bedroom, I saw that the name card on my bedroom door had been removed, folded, and slid halfway under the door. In my room, I closed the door and unfolded the paper: "Theresa," it said. "I'm sorry about leaving you tonight. Come upstairs as soon as you read this. We need to talk.—Debbie."

I found my way to her door, hesitated, and knocked.

"Come up," Debbie called. I tried the knob; it was unlocked.

I went up the narrow staircase and stepped onto a storey that was a near replica of the second floor, except that it looked lived in, like a real home. End tables with piles of books were pushed up against the wall of the hall; a long carpet ran down the length of the hall floor. Pictures of birds and animals and people were framed and hung on the walls.

Instruments sat in stands or in cases propped against tables. A record was on, and the low metallic notes of what I could only guess was a harpsichord or a thumb piano plucked at the silence. The room to the right, the equivalent of the master bedroom on the second floor, was set up like a sitting room. There was a space heater placed inside the fireplace. Lamps were set on crates and desks and tables. Debbie sat on an armchair by the fireplace.

"Hi," she said. "Sorry about leaving you with Grant. I needed to get away, even if it meant leaving you, which I didn't want to do. Here, have a seat. And have this. You earned it." She handed me a glass of wine that was sitting on the floor by her chair. It looked like the one she had taken with her to bed.

"I think I'm okay," I said. "Thanks." I sat down in the chair across from her.

"I'm not sure how he managed to set things up this way. I came home from college and here he was, acting like Allen Jr., running the show. But God love him if he could connect with Allen. Mr. Poole was not a kind man. He taught me to love music. I'm grateful to him for that, and for my education. But it's hard to feel warm toward someone who didn't like people."

"Do you think Grant is representing what Mr. Poole wanted done with his money?" I asked.

"What Allen Poole loved were houses, buildings. He loved the academy building, the grand look of an old school. He couldn't stand to see what had become of it, the jewel of the town. He didn't want people to hang out in the academy's chapel, didn't want kids to play road hockey on the tile floor of the old gym. People were already lighting fires in the buildings. The Big Fire must have struck him as a story that people would believe. I could never prove it, but my mom always said she thought Poole set that fire himself. We'll never know. But I know Grant is a lot like him. Burning things down is similar to building them up, if either is done on a big enough scale. They're different forms of starting over. Neither of them, Grant or Allen, see people; they see the business of space."

I paused, not sure exactly what she was implying, not really wanting to get further involved. The focus for me wasn't on the history but the present, the meaning of this job Debbie and I were to share and how I could confirm that this had been a mistake.

"Why are you working for Grant?" I asked.

She shrugged. "He called and offered me the job. I was done school, and had no other prospects. My room was still here as I'd left it. This attic. My mom and I lived here briefly after Allen died, until I went away and she moved in with her boyfriend in the country. She was ready to go. She already practically lived here while he was alive; she did all his cleaning, some of his cooking. At least now I have an ally, now that you're here. It will be fun to live together. We can go for walks. Grant was right about that. Alden is a great place for walking. The train tracks are amazing; they've become like an orchard planted in lines, with fruit trees growing in the ditches on either side. You can smell them. That's why I keep the window open."

But I knew I wasn't going to stay, if I could find a way of refusing a free place to live. The faint smell of overly sweet, slightly fermented fruit wafted into the room on the breeze, or maybe it was just Debbie's words that made me think it did. As much as I needed the job, it wasn't a good fit. The post shouldn't have been vacant in the first place. And I couldn't forget what he said; it had seemed to come not from him, but channelled from somewhere—from Allen the belated misanthrope, or maybe, rather, from Alden's buildings themselves, talking back. The communication was welcome, despite the vehicle. Most likely, I'd give it a few days and see how it turned out, keeping in mind that the train station was just a half-hour cab ride away. I'd give it a few days because walking away wasn't going to be as easy this time.

INSIDE CITY HALL

THREE MONTHS INTO MY NEW JOB IN THE CITY HALL'S HR department, I started receiving strange calls from an unknown caller on my office phone.

Five months in, the calls had become so frequent that the fact of them—avoiding them, inadvertently answering them, thinking about them—had become as much a part of the workday as going for more coffee, checking the time, or meeting with my co-workers. Very quickly, I began to know, almost always, when I was going to hear her voice, that voice, when I picked up the phone.

But sometimes I was wrong. Sometimes I would answer the phone with my guard down, as I rushed in from a meeting, or grabbed the receiver, expecting a call from someone else. I would reel off my professional greeting, only to hear her deep voice on the other end, answering mine with her own equally formal greeting: "Hello, and good morning," or "Hello, and good afternoon."

She called from different phone numbers almost every time. I kept a list on a sticky note, jotting the digits from the phone's display screen, while I listened to the caller talk, or while I sat, watching the ringing phone until it fell silent. The only information I could gather on her was that ever-growing list of numbers.

This may have been part of the reason I'd avoided telling anyone else in the office about the calls. I knew I needed to tell my executive officer, Adair, about what was going on, but I'd avoided having that talk with him, oddly, almost to the same extent that I'd tried to avoid conversations with the caller herself. I didn't want to talk to the caller: her calls were confusing and irritating; more importantly, they had begun taking up a fair bit of my time at work. But Adair and his wife had just had their first babies—twins. Managers and co-workers crowded into his office doorway each day, around the desk of the sleepless, always-working Adair, to look at the most recent pictures of the girls on his computer or phone. I didn't want to be the one to push through, parting and silencing the smiling crowd, to announce that we had a situation in the office. Especially since he'd taken a chance on me, and I'd started so recently. His professionalism and intelligent smile made me feel professional and intelligent, and I wanted to coast on that for a while without making things weird.

I told my brother about the situation, and he surprised me by responding not with sympathy for me, but with the judgment that I had been putting my whole office and myself at risk by not telling anyone: what if this person—this caller—came in, out of control, and someone got hurt? I didn't want to have to reveal to my office, after the fact, that I'd been assisting a threatening outside force. But it became easier to just avoid the caller's calls and deal with them when I had to. I was banking on my gut feeling that she was harmless, and just didn't understand the normal process for seeking a job, which I sympathized with, because these days it seemed like the process had grown so complicated and competitive that only people with direct training or experience really understood it.

Adair had generously hired me to work in the POD office (Professional & Organizational Development), within the HR department of city hall, as a professional development resources coordinator, even though my college diploma in human resources that qualified me for the new position was still in progress, part-time. At my interview, Adair had let me make much of my two previous jobs. After completing a university undergraduate degree in theatre studies, and then a college diploma in career counselling, I'd worked for a few years at that same college's Career Resource Centre, as a career resource advisor for students. After quitting that job, I'd started at city hall, where I'd been working on contract in a low-level administrative role in the mayor's office when Adair hired me.

I think the way Adair and I met had helped my case: I'd called him and asked him if he would be willing to do an information-gathering interview with me, to give me a chance to ask him questions about his profession. He later said that this move had made a strong impression on him.

The PDR coordinator position came with a raise and heightened responsibility. Its main function was to coordinate professional development workshops for other city employees. But, with my hire, the POD office was also launching a new pilot project: versions of these PDR workshops would be opened up to the public, and not just to city employees.

I liked the new job. Coordinating was like stage-managing.

My role was to plan the workshops; book the expert speakers—authors, consultants, or professors I knew from the college—who led the sessions; book rooms; and promote the sessions. On the day of each workshop, I would greet the participants, make sure the AV equipment cooperated, and see that discussions remained on track and respectful. I liked the sessions that were open to my fellow city employees, but I liked those intended for the public more. Any time members of the public walked into and through my professional world in city hall I felt as though the building was breathing and I was floating on that breath.

My office in the POD wing of the HR department of city hall had one small window overlooking the building's huge, charcoal-coloured stone mezzanine, where people walk, carrying paperwork, umbrellas, or bagged lunches. The office was small, but it had a door I could close, with a nameplate beside it.

I'm almost certain that my caller initially encountered me at the first professional development session we offered that was open to the public, a workshop titled "The Information-Gathering Interview: Just the Facts, Ma'am."

I say that she encountered me, as opposed to us encountering each other, because I'd been at a disadvantage on the day of the workshop. My nerves had flared that morning when I checked the registration list and saw just how many people had signed up to come. And most of them did turn up. I stood at the door of the carpeted meeting room, greeting each registrant as they arrived, repeating each name as it evaporated from my brain. I invited people to help themselves to coffee, straightened the sugar packets beside the carafe, and offered Brad, my HR colleague and that day's speaker, a second coffee. Donna was there too. She was another cause of my nerves.

It had taken some gumption to ask Donna, my former boss in the mayor's office, before Adair, to come by the session and offer me feedback at the end of it, from her perspective as a communications expert. But she quickly agreed.

The topic of the workshop had been my idea. Though I hadn't learned the term for it until recently, the concept was familiar to me, in practice. In fact, I got both of my jobs with the city though information-gathering interviews.

It was my friend Kai, my former colleague at the Career Resource Centre at the college, who suggested the idea to me. Before getting in at the city, I'd begun to regret quitting my job at the college. I was applying for jobs indiscriminately and with growing desperation, without a bite. I told Kai about it over a drink at a dark Irish pub downtown.

"Why don't you just try reaching out to someone to ask for information?" he asked. "Just choose somewhere you'd like to work. Do a search online for someone at the organization who has a title you'd like to have, and then email them to ask if they'd be willing to talk to you on the phone. The key is, they'll be flattered. Everyone likes being asked about themselves. You can ask them about what skills, knowledge, and credentials they found relevant going into their own position, and what steps they'd recommend to someone hoping to break into that field. It turns the tables, because it's like you're interviewing them. It releases the desire, to be chosen by you, inside of them." This seemed a bit Machiavellian to me, but I was in no position not to try it.

Kai had apparently been right about it; he usually was right—except when he'd said there was no reason we couldn't go on working together at the college despite our on-again-off-again office romance, which had carried us around the hidden spaces of the college campus, into back halls, and empty classrooms. Once, an embrace was interrupted, just in time, as our elevator opened and our boss stepped in.

What bothered me about the situation with Kai at the college was that it always felt like we were acting, or at least I was, playing out an office-romance script we'd both seen or read. I left the job at the Career Centre not exactly because of the romance. Rather, it was because of what my choice to initiate and pursue it, despite how unprofessional it was—how unfair it was to Kai and to myself—told me about how stimulating I was finding the job. But Kai was a good person, and a source of valued support in my life. After leaving, I continued meeting up with him semi-regularly for drinks or coffee.

My first information-gathering interview at the city had been with Donna in the mayor's office, where she worked as a communications director. I sat on the phone looking through the rain-spattered window of my apartment and took notes as she spoke. Donna's laugh made me picture handfuls of diamonds and gold being poured into a mixed pile. I drew sketches of diamond rings in the corner of my notebook. By the end of our conversation, Donna said, "You know, if you're interested, there's a position coming up in our office that we're just about to post. It's an admin position. But if you're interested in getting in at city hall, you should apply." I did apply, and I got the job.

Once I was in the position, installed in my cubicle on a

carpeted, brightly lit wing that looked unrelated to the dark, stone halls outside of it, on a quiet afternoon, I picked up the phone and called Adair. I told him I was earning an HR diploma at the college, and already had diplomas in career counselling and theatre studies, and asked if we could meet so that I could ask some questions about his area of work. We met for the conversation. I was starting to feel bad, especially because Donna was so kind, and Adair was so kind. I couldn't forget how manipulative and opportunistic I'd thought the information-gathering interview had sounded when Kai told me about it, and I felt insincere. But at the same time I did sincerely enjoy talking to them, and I did gather information. It was part of bypassing the bureaucracy, I guessed, to get through to the way things really work—through human connection, the human part of Human Resources. I just wished I felt more human doing it.

The subtitle of the information-gathering interview workshop—"Just the Facts, Ma'am"—had come from Adair's boss, Ryan. Ryan had dropped in on Adair and me in Adair's office when we were reviewing the plan for the session. He looked at the mock-up of our poster, with its graphic of merging conversation bubbles, and asked, "Why not lighten things up? God knows things are gloomy enough in this place." He had a point. City hall was a massive, modern, severe building made of huge blocks of shiny, imported, dark-grey stone— the building's nickname among locals and employees alike was the Monolith.

"You're talking about getting information," Ryan said. "Facts, right? 'Just the facts, ma'am.' Make a joke. That's allowed, you know. Make it like a mock detective story. Have some fun with it."

Donna loved the session's title. I met her for coffee to ask her if she'd be willing to sit in on the workshop to give me feedback and answer questions that came up that she could speak to. "The facts, ma'am. Just the facts," she repeated, laughing. It was the kind of phrase people can't resist repeating if they hear it spoken; they long to play that part, just for a second. And Donna, I couldn't help but note, was perfect for the role, with her tendency to wear raincoats and carry briefcases, and her curly black hair that hung around her head; she was a combination of femme fatale and hardboiled detective, compounded by the aura of authority projected by her age—she was in her late fifties—and her casual articulateness.

The day of the workshop, Brad, the speaker, and Donna both arrived early, and we sat in the meeting room I'd booked, at one end of the long table, chatting.

The session, expectedly, went really well. Brad came unprepared, with no AV props or a script, but it just became a conversation, and Donna chimed in with great advice, even though she came from outside Human Resources. She was funny and relaxed, easily engaging the participants. A mother of three was looking to get back into the workforce in a new field now that her kids were in school; a quiet woman said she had studied art history and was now looking to get a job in city art programming; a man in his fifties had been working at a call centre and said he couldn't take one more week of it; a backdrop of hazier faces and voices filled out the conversation with sincere and mutually affirming commiserations, confessions, and expressions of concern. They were a balanced, mixed group, all pleasant enough not to have stood out much in my mind following the session, as I headed back to my office with the box of coffee dregs and the papers on which I'd taken notes about the apparent needs of the public regarding the job search.

I'd thanked Donna in the hall outside the meeting room, with sincere gratitude, and she leaned in and gave me a hug. My mind, as I headed back into my own wing, felt like foil, catching light and flinging it around, as I unlocked my office door, closed it, and sat at my desk. I scrolled through email with unfocused eyes, and then gazed at the picture I kept on my desk beside the phone: a framed black-and-white picture of my maternal grandmother and her sister as teenagers. In the picture, my grandmother stands on a seawall with a fishing rod in one hand. Below her, her sister lies in the fetal position, and one of my grandmother's feet is planted triumphantly on her sister's hip, as though the sister is a record game fish my grandmother has just caught. Both girls are laughing, their hair and skirts windswept, impervious to the stormy sea or sky behind them. I keep this picture on my desk in any job because it makes for interesting conversations, and it's a way of showing something about who I am at work.

I took a sandwich from my desk drawer and settled in for a few moments of glassiness while I ate. It was at that moment that the phone rang. I picked up the receiver on the first ring, thinking it would be Donna calling about a thought generated for her by the morning's workshop, or Adair calling to ask how the workshop had gone.

"Hello, Office of Professional and Organizational Development. Katherine speaking. How can I help you?" I asked.

"Yes. I have some questions about seeking employment with the city," a voice said. It was slightly difficult to hear her. Her voice was loud, as though she was holding the receiver close to her mouth, and there was background noise, what sounded like cars driving in rain or people swishing by, behind her. I could hear the metallic coiling of a ribbed cord, like she was calling from a pay phone and shifting from foot to foot.

"Sure. I'm happy to try to help," I said. "I offer guidance about PD resources, not specific to employment with the city, but if I can help, I'm glad to. What would you like to know?"

"I have a cousin. She's never worked much, because she's been...unavailable for work. Could she get a job with your office?"

"Well...that would depend. I generally can't give information about specific opportunities to work here. But maybe if you tell me about her skills and interests, I can offer some general ideas."

"What I want to know is...a job for her inside city hall. Would this be possible, or not possible? You can just let me know frankly. I know you're busy. I don't want to take up all your time."

"You see, I can't answer the question if I don't know anything more about her or what type of position she's looking for."

"She's highly educated."

"Okay, great. What kind of job do you think she would be interested in? What field of study did she focus on?"

"She focused on psychology. She has an advanced degree, but now she's interested in management. She would hope to earn a certain amount of money. Would you say this is possible, or not possible? Inside city hall?"

"Well, I would have to say, maybe possible. But unlikely."

"Unlikely?"

"Yes. Possible because she's educated in psychology, which

could be relevant to certain types of management. But unlikely because, as you said, she doesn't have much work experience. But there are lots of things she can do—"

"What credentials will she need to have?"

"I'm sorry, I can't answer generically without knowing what particular job she's interested in applying for and what credentials she already has."

"She has a master's in organizational psychology. She would be interested in a job as a director or manager. She's an ideas person. Do you think it's possible? Or is it not possible?"

"Not possible," I said. I hated saying it, but I had to draw the conversation to a close and I was not prepared to offer misleading information that would give either this woman or her cousin false hopes.

"Hello?" I said. The dial tone buzzed in my ear, and I realized the caller had hung up.

I came to expect the calls, which came a few times a week, and then a few times a day. Initially, my automatic reaction was to close the door before picking up the phone when I thought it was her, as though our conversations were secret. I felt anxious that if she had been a participant at my workshop on the information-gathering interview, her reaction to and use of what she'd learned there was the ultimate indicator that I hadn't planned it well, that it hadn't been useful, and that I wasn't good at my job. I couldn't forget that I'd forgotten the names of all the participants I'd met at the workshop. I hadn't been quite myself that day.

She became increasingly frank when she called, asking, always, that black-or-white question: possible, or not possible? Saying, always, that she didn't want to take up my time. The fifth time she called, she introduced a new theme, in response to the frustration in my voice when I told her that

I didn't feel that I could help her or that she was contacting the appropriate person with her queries.

"The wisdom of your soul is a pearl beyond price," she said. "You're angry because you want to help, because you have a priceless wisdom—a wise spirit." This expression and variants of it became a staple of her comments when she called, especially when I was curt with her.

The cousin she was asking on behalf of became her sister, then herself—hypothetically for herself, she said. Was I hiring? Was my boss hiring? When I told her I didn't have the power to hire, she asked if someone she called the boss was hiring.

"Donna?" I asked.

"The elegant one. The higher-up. The one who gave some of the information at the interview. More information than the man leading it."

"The tall one?"

"Yes."

"That's Donna. I don't know if she's hiring. But the best way to find out if a job is available anywhere with the city is to look at the job postings on the city website."

"In the interview when I met you, the woman with the information said the best way to find a job is to call," she said.

"It wasn't an interview. It was a workshop on information-gathering interviews."

"I'm calling because I have some information about myself to run by you, assuming I were to apply for a job. The woman from the workshop may have the information, but I would argue that a candidate like myself has information too. A candidate like you, with your soul's wisdom and your ideas. The city needs facts, but it also needs ideas. Wisdom is beyond price."

"Facts? Ideas?" I said. I didn't want to discuss my own approach or my own qualities as an employee or thinker.

"Sometimes I think you're not there to give information, but to hoard it. Maybe you want to keep your pearls to yourself, because you know they give you power."

"I'm sorry, I have another call and I need to go." I hung up the phone, opened the door to my office, and went down the hall to see Ryan. Adair's boss. I didn't want to make Adair deal with this. He always ended up dealing with everything that came up.

"Ryan's at a conference. You're not the only one looking for him, believe me. Can I help you with something?" Jude, the administrative assistant who served all the managers in the office, sat at a desk beside Adair's office.

"Jude, do you have a number for security?"

"Why, Katherine? Is something wrong? If there is, please let me know. I need to know."

"Oh, it's nothing. I've just been getting some annoying calls."

"What kind of calls?"

"They're just strange and they're interrupting my work. I'm hoping to block the number. You know what it's like." I didn't feel like explaining what was going on because I was embarrassed I'd let it go on so long.

"Oh, I see what you mean," Jude said. "Yup, here's the number. They'll block his calls for you. Watch out, though. The spell will just deepen." Jude was thinking of a theory she had that Kai was under my spell. I'd never bothered to explain that it wasn't a spell but instead a kind of ingrained pattern that bound the two of us, me to him and him to me.

Kai had come in looking for me one day, without calling me in advance. I'd come back from lunch and he was waiting on the bench against the wall beside Jude's desk, across from Adair's open office door. Jude had given me a look that asked, "Do you want me to call you into a 'meeting'?" I shook my head, winked, and smiled, implying that he was okay. Since then, Jude had taunted me about my gentleman caller; the running joke was that Kai had love potion on his eyes. Jude was in a production of *A Midsummer Night's Dream* with the amateur theatre company that puts on plays in the square in front of city hall in the summer. Kai actually did call sometimes, but not too much. I'd let Jude run with the joke.

Back in my office, I called security and explained the situation. They said they would look into it and get back to me.

There was a knock on my office door. I opened it, expecting to see Jude, but it was Kai.

"Hi," he said. "Do you have a minute?"

"Sure," I said. "Come in."

"Do you have time to go for a walk?" he said. I remembered that Adair was out of the office. I felt very tired, like I could hardly stand. I closed the door behind him.

"Lie down with me for a minute," I said. I took his hand and pushed the chair out of the way and we dropped together to the floor, as my phone started to ring on my desk. I pictured Donna, her hair wet in the rain of the fall day, and her raincoated silhouette, the solidity of her being, and I closed my eyes until the ringing stopped. I pulled one of Kai's arms around me.

"Katherine. I can't. I have to go. I have an interview." Kai's voice was too loud, his breath blowing the hairs against my ear.

"An interview?" I said, opening my eyes and looking at his, about two inches from mine.

"Well, an information exchange, I guess, is a better way to describe it. A conversation."

"With who?"

"With your old boss. Donna. They're creating a new team, possibly hiring a few new people, a kind of big-picture consultancy committee, for rethinking how the city interacts with the public. I thought for sure you'd be part of the meeting. That's why I came by."

The phone rang on the desk again. I needed to get up anyway. I hoped it would be Donna, inviting me to come talk to her about what Kai was describing.

"Hello?" I said.

"Hi, Katherine? It's security again. Just calling to let you know that we're working on this issue. Hopefully we can figure out where these calls are coming from. For now, though, be safe and let us know if you want a walk off the property later on."

"Okay," I said. "Thanks. But I'm pretty sure this person is just looking for information about her job search. It's my job to help with that. She just doesn't quite get how things work."

"Nonetheless, we need to be better safe than sorry, okay? This doesn't mean you go without pay. It just means you stay safe. Work should be a safe place."

"That sounds creepy, Kath," Kai said, when I'd explained it all to him. "Why didn't you tell me you were getting those calls? Did you tell anyone? I think it's clearly better if you go home. If this woman is in the building and she's calling you repeatedly, there's a word for that."

"I know," I said.

"Okay, but it's true. And it's not your fault."

"Of course I know it's not my fault," I said. "Why would it be my fault?"

"Donna said you've seemed stressed lately. Now I understand why."

"Donna said that?"

"Well, not in words. But she said she cares about you, and I got the feeling she was worried."

"Do you think that's why I wasn't invited to this meeting?"

"I have no idea why you weren't. I know you were worried because you used the information-gathering strategy to get in with her, and then used it to leave soon after, but I never thought she would have any problem with that. She's a pro herself and knows how things work."

"I want to be on that committee. I need to stop hoarding information and share it. That's the big-picture idea I have to offer."

"Okay, well, I'll tell Donna what's happening and ask if I can reschedule another time to meet with her. And I'll ask if you can come with me. The rest of them can go ahead today. For now, I'll go with you."

"No," I said. "That isn't necessary. I'll take a cab. I'll be fine." I didn't want Kai coming over, didn't want the afternoon to lead to an evening, the prospect of drinking a bottle of wine together, the rain against the window an excuse for him to stay, falling asleep together on my couch, then morning and the unknown.

I walked out of my office, gestured for him to follow me out, and thanked him for coming in a professional tone, so my neighbouring colleagues would think we'd been in a meeting. We walked together out to the hall, and then to the elevators. He hugged me as I waited for the elevator to rise to my floor. I stepped into the elevator alone, and as it closed between us Kai leaned his head toward me and raised an eyebrow, lifting one hand to his ear with his three central fingers folded in and the pinky and thumb outstretched, the shape of the kind of old receiver phone we know from movies and childhood, the platonic form of the telephone that hangs above us in the sky like a star-sized disco ball, littering the universe with myriad moving fragments of itself.

When the elevator doors opened, I could see that it was raining again, as it had been for most of the fall. The custodian who mopped up the water tracked in daily now by comers and goers stood still, ahead of me, his back to me, in the centre of the dark, high-ceilinged mezzanine, looking outside at the deepening grey and blue of the early evening beyond the glass doors, with one foot on the locked wheel of his bucket and one arm resting on his mop, a visual echo of my grandmother's triumphal pose in the picture in my office, but empty of the drama that charges any shared tableau.

In the mezzanine, the overhead lights that flicker on only in response to your steps, to save power, left me solely illuminated just outside the elevator. The custodian was so still that his lights had gone out; he could have been a statue, shadowed by the walls' mammoth blocks of shiny stone. A pay phone stood against the wall on the far side of the open hall. Its metal cord gleamed. Now that my eyes had adjusted, one other figure emerged, sitting against this same far wall. A woman sat waiting on a bench near the glass doors that led to the elevators up to Donna's office. She wore a tailored raincoat, and an umbrella sat folded at her feet. She sat perfectly still, in rapt concentration, studying a notebook in her lap.

FORTIFIED WINE

WHEN MY FRIEND RICHARD GOT THE NEWS THAT HE would be moving to Maine to take a two-month-long painting master class, he offered to let me stay at his apartment while he was gone. I'd been wanting to leave my apartment anyway, because the building was for sale and prospective owners were always coming through to look at it. It was good timing. And I could keep an eye on Richard's art for him, which would bring him peace of mind. We'd been friends since we were kids; we'd both grown up in the same mid-sized town and both moved to the nearest big city, in his case to go to art school, and in my case for a job in fundraising for an art gallery, which I'd left soon after; I'd been drifting from job to job since then.

Richard left me a note on the hall table under a bottle of wine, telling me how glad he was that I'd be keeping his paintings and sculptures safe, and staying in his place. The brand of the wine he left me on top of the note was Vera—my first name.

Richard had never actually had a break-in. But his apartment had a slightly unnerving story to it, which he'd explained still made him slightly nervous about leaving it unoccupied. One night a few days after he had first moved in, about two years back, he'd been reading on his couch and noticed a trail of smoke rising past his back window. He got up and looked out the window, down into the alley behind the building, and saw a stranger. This stranger had been sitting and smoking halfway up the fire escape that led to his balcony.

The next night, she was sitting there again, in the same place, and then again later that week. He hadn't seen her face, but had noted her coat, its unique shade of green, the way her hair spread in a fan across the coat's shoulders, the solid, still way she sat, her lifting and lowering arm holding the cigarette. And then, after not seeing her for a few nights, he saw her again. In the street, during the day. In front of his place, in the same coat, with the same hair, ahead of him, walking away, quickly. And then she was gone. Though he hadn't seen the woman since that time, he still mentioned her occasionally; I could tell that as much as he seemed to like having the story to tell, he had never felt entirely comfortable in his apartment, or leaving it empty, because of it.

Richard's apartment was quiet and full of art. I spent my first few nights there alone, sipping tea in silence on his low, green couch, looking at his paintings and sculptures, his curtains and knick-knacks, the lamplight coloured by tinted lampshades. I marvelled at how cozy solitude could feel, away from the company of my own possessions, which I'd moved with me from place to place since university, and which now sat in storage on the other side of the city, along with some items I was saving to sell.

Richard was a slightly distant person who kept to himself, and I had never fully felt able to trust him, despite how long we'd known each other. But I'd accepted our quiet friendship for what it was. He had accepted me as I was too, despite some bad choices I'd made in recent years. When I'd had to leave my last job, he got me a job at the department store where his father was a manager; I'd walk the fluorescent aisles, picking up clothes that had fallen from their hangers, and direct people to the sections they were looking for. Richard would come by and visit me, and eat with me in the food court of the mall. I'd left shortly after I began, but it had helped a lot. Now, I accepted Richard's offer to stay at his apartment with a bodily relief about my own finances that carried me like new strength, letting me walk faster and pick objects up with less effort: my things, Richard's things, pen and paper for planning. I felt closer to Richard with him gone than I ever had when he was here.

My fifth evening at Richard's place after he left, I sat on his couch drinking the last of the bottle of Vera wine he'd left me, writing up a to-do list including a sublist of places I wanted to visit to try to sell things: books, some gold jewellery I'd been given as gifts in the past, a few pieces of art that I'd bought when I had a better-paying office job, my first good salary. One of these items I was thinking of selling was a piece of art that Richard had given me—not his work, but one of the sculptures his grandmother had made and left to him. I still hadn't decided if I was going to sell it or not. But it made me uneasy, so I'd always kept it in a box.

Richard's grandmother had been a somewhat well-known artist, at least in her own city, in her day. She did sculptures—in a range of sizes, from a half-foot high to waist-high—of abstract human figures metamorphosing into something else. Each sculpture was named for the thing the figure was becoming: water, light, sound, love, fear, air, loss, truth. The one Richard had given me was titled *Truth*. It was a small one, only about as long as my forearm, of a woman with her arms reaching up to cover her face. He'd given it to me because my name, Vera, means truth, he explained. I think the figure's posture was supposed to represent truth's hiddenness, but to me she just looked scared. I preferred the others, which showed people transforming into tangible things like water or light, rather than into abstract concepts.

The sculpture was in a shoebox in my storage unit, and I'd begun to look into places that might be interested in buying it, though I was afraid Richard would somehow find out if I did sell it. I didn't want to hurt his feelings. But I also couldn't help but notice how just one drop of allegory spreads and permeates everything around it; the sculpture seemed to come with its own built-in defence: if you put a figure representing truth in a box to get away from its heavy-handed metaphor, you end up making it even more heavy-handed.

Richard himself worked in oil paint and his work was abstract, focused on light and colour. His paintings all had the same title, *Stained Glass*, followed by a number. One of his paintings served as the central focus of his living room—*Stained Glass Nine*. It consisted of ten partially overlapping squares in shades of green, amber, and yellow, along with some vertical lines of magenta running through it like spindly veins of mercury in glass. The first night I'd sat in the apartment, I spent some time looking at it and had trouble understanding the appeal. That evening, though, when I looked up at it again from the page covered with my to-do list, I was struck in a new way by the colours and how they offset each other to create an effect of paned light. The painting itself looked like a window, and I began to appreciate it.

My phone buzzed against the fabric of the couch cushion beside me, signalling a text. "Safely arrived. Thanks again." It was from Richard. The time read 7:02 p.m.

At that moment, like a deeper echo of the buzz of my phone, a loud buzz rang out from the apartment's front hall. The front-door buzzer. In the hall, I pressed the intercom button and said, "Hello?" but no response. So, I slipped my shoes on, stuck one of Richard's boots in the door to hold it open, and went down to the door that opened onto the street. A woman in a white parka, with the hood pulled partly back from her face, stood there holding an illuminated tablet computer in her bare hand in the cold, her boots planted in the salted ice. She smiled.

"Hi," she said. "I came by before and spoke to Richard."

"Hi," I said. "How are you?" I wasn't sure if this was a friend of Richard's or some kind of salesperson, and I wasn't sure what tone to take.

"I'm doing well, thanks. How have you been?"

"I've been well, thanks." I wasn't sure if I should tell her I was housesitting for Richard; I hesitated to reveal any information without checking with him.

"I'm not sure if Richard might have mentioned this, but I'm here because of this." She raised her hand holding the tablet, and the screen threw a rectangle of light toward me. I saw that passages on the screen were highlighted in yellow. "The Bible. Richard and I met in the neighbourhood and he said he was interested in some reading and discussion sessions about the scripture's meaning. He said he was going to be travelling—to Massachusetts, I think? I was hoping to catch him before he left. I've chosen some passages. He was telling me he does paintings of church windows, I think? I've tried to choose some passages that he might find interesting."

She gestured again with her tablet, and I saw the capitalized word "Light" in one of the yellow-highlighted sections. She was attractive in a not-obvious way, with a high forehead and large eyes. I found it hard to believe that Richard had really agreed to a reading session, but she appeared to express no doubt about that, even as she seemed nervous in other ways. As she spoke, she tugged at the cord of her jacket's hood with one hand. Maybe Richard hadn't realized she was a religious solicitor, if that was indeed what she was.

"I'm sorry. Richard isn't here," I said. The instinctive cross between sympathy and impatience that I feel when trapped with any salesperson or solicitor was making me fidget with anxiety—but she looked slightly forlorn, like this wasn't easy for her, so I tried not to be rude.

"Oh, that's no trouble," she said. "I can come back sometime soon."

"Do you have his number? If not, I can check with him..."

"No, but I don't mind coming by another time. I'm in the neighbourhood. Can I ask your name?"

"Vera," I said.

"Okay, well, you have a nice night, Vera. Here," she said. She took a notebook and wrote her name on it. "Cheri—Bible discussion," it said, followed by a phone number. "I'm Cheri. It's pronounced 'Sherry,' like the wine."

"Thanks, Cheri," I said. I closed the door and went back upstairs, wondering if I should have either discouraged her or been more friendly. To be safe, I thought I should check in with Richard to make sure everything was on the up-and-up and there were no miscommunications.

"Richard," I texted him. "Sorry to bother you. A woman

just came by and I want to ask how you'd like me to deal with her."

My phone rang a moment later.

"Vera, is everything okay?" He sounded tired. "Did something happen?"

"Oh, everything is totally fine," I said. "A woman named Cheri came by. She said you'd talked to her about having a Bible-study discussion with her or something... Don't tell me you've converted and forgot to mention it."

"Oh. Her."

"She's evangelical, I think," I said.

"I can't figure out what group she's a part of. You know what, though? She seems nice. We talked for a while one evening about church windows. She was out front, and I think she was going door-to-door. She said hi and we ended up talking. She's actually pretty insightful. I thought, why not give her a chance?"

I didn't say anything, but I thought—plus, she's pretty, regardless of her faith or its motive. I still wasn't sure if Richard had romantic relationships with people of any gender identity—he seemed only to have friends, as far as I could see, and I wasn't sure if any of those friendships went deeper, but I'd watched his eyes appreciate various human forms.

"When you texted, I thought you meant that woman from the fire escape had come back. I freaked out a bit. I shouldn't have called. I think I just need some sleep."

"What would you like me to do about Cheri? Is it okay if I tell her you're away?"

"It is," he said. "I already told her I was going away, all about the master class, my work. She's harmless. Don't let her convert you, though. She seems like she could be persuasive."

I told him to try to sleep and we hung up. I lay down on

top of the quilt on Richard's bed. Against the wall opposite was a chest on which sat one of his grandmother's sculptures: *Water*. I liked that one: an upright human figure's legs spread into a circular, rippling pool that formed the sculpture's base; the fluid-shaped body looked like it was pouring down into the pool. I liked it a lot more than *Truth*. For the first time, I wondered if Richard might have given me that *Truth* sculpture not because of the connection to my name, but because he didn't like it, and wanted to give it away. If so, I wouldn't feel as bad selling it.

I fell asleep trying to picture his grandmother's workroom: its plastic-draped tables strewn with flakes of stone, and metal tools; the sound of chisels cutting negative space away from a stone shape; voices and faces moving through the room admiring her work, and seeking to tempt her gaze away from her still figures toward their moving forms.

I spent the next day moving around in Richard's apartment, from the couch to the table to the kitchen. It was mid-winter, and the cold snap continued, with more snow that had fallen overnight. I stayed inside, making myself snacks and cups of instant coffee from a jar in Richard's cupboard. The light outside, reflected from the snow, was brilliant that afternoon, and the whole apartment looked bigger, brighter, and more cheerful than it had the night before.

As four-thirty approached, the last hour of light, Richard's painting, *Stained Glass Nine*, caught my eye. It looked brighter, somehow, though it had just started getting darker outside, and I realized that the sensation of brightness in the apartment earlier that day had been partially an effect of the painting fading into the background. The painting's light was dark, viscous, and set off, jewel-like, by the darkening sky.

An hour later, I realized I'd only eaten cheese and crackers and apples that day. I rummaged through the cupboards again. At the back of one I saw a tall bottle with a black-and-white label, and pulled it out. It was a full bottle of a dark, brownish-red alcohol that looked like port or sherry. "Oloroso del Puerto," the label said in curlicued letters. I put it back in the cupboard, remembering that I should never drink, not even a sip, on an empty stomach. I decided that no matter the cold, I would have to go to the grocery store for some real food. I put on my coat and went down to the street.

When I stepped outside, I was surprised to see Cheri standing there on the sidewalk, a couple of feet away. She was talking to someone, another woman. I wonder if I can run past them? I thought. Or go back inside. But when Cheri saw me, she waved and smiled at me, and the other woman waved at her and walked away.

"Hi, Vera!" she said. "I was just coming by to see you. Is Richard around by any chance? Have you heard from him?"

"Richard says hi," I said. "I talked to him. He's in Maine. He'll be away for a while."

"Oh, well," she said. "I hope he has a wonderful trip. It must be snowy there too, though. It gets dark early these days, doesn't it?"

"It does," I said. "I was just on my way to get some groceries. I didn't eat much today."

"I was thinking I might eat out somewhere tonight. Have you been to the place on the corner? They have good food. You're welcome to join me."

I'd noticed the place on the corner, although I hadn't been sure if it was a nightclub or a bar or a restaurant. The windows looking in were tinted to appear almost opaque, and you could see only outlines of objects inside.

"Okay," I said. I scanned my mind for any reason I could give for saying no. I could say I couldn't afford it, which was true, but I heard myself saying yes before I could say no. I was too hungry to think straight, and again I noticed that she looked slightly sad and nervous, and I felt bad leaving her, despite my anxiety about entering into conversations about religion.

We walked together through the dark door into a small, slightly dingy pub with one pool table in the middle of the room, and sat at a table near the window. A woman in a tight black dress came and took our order—steak and fries. Cheri ordered for herself, and I asked for the same, not wanting to think about the decision.

"And wine," said Cheri. "Some wine would be nice. What do you think?" she asked.

"A litre or half-litre?" asked the woman in the black dress.

"A litre," Cheri said. "That's okay, right," she said to me, and I nodded. I felt trapped by the wine. I didn't expect her to be a drinker, and I felt uneasy drinking with her, fearing I might let my guard down and enter into a conversation about the Bible that could only become insincere or argumentative on my end. But I also really wanted a drink.

The steak was simple and pretty good. I was famished, and ate it quickly. Cheri hardly touched hers, and I ate my fries as she drank her wine.

"Have you been in the neighbourhood for long?" she asked.

"No. I don't really know this neighbourhood. I'm just house-sitting for Richard," I said.

"I grew up in this neighbourhood. But it feels like I'm getting to know it for the first time. I've gone through a bit of a life event over the last few years and the world looks pretty new in general. Different."

I wasn't sure if this was a reference to a religious awakening or not. I tried to keep things general. She told me about the street where she'd grown up, not far from there, and the big trees on it with curving branches that she said she liked looking up at from her bedroom window. She said she'd spent a lot of time in bed because of a health problem that had changed things for her.

She looked down, and I worried for a moment that she was crying, but she looked back up and seemed composed.

"But it's had a few silver linings. I've spent a lot of time reading, and learning about things I never cared about before. That's part of why Richard and I connected. We're interested in some of the same things—stained glass, especially. Actually, part of why I wanted to see Richard is because I wanted to ask him something."

"What's that?"

"I wanted to ask him if he knows that stained glass was once known as 'the poor man's Bible.' I wondered if he was already intending to convey God's ideas in his work."

I paused and looked down at my hands. The direct refocusing onto religion had come up so suddenly that I was taken off guard. And I began to wonder if she'd seen his paintings, and whether she'd been in his apartment, and if so, when and how.

"Richard definitely talks like an artist. You know what he told me? He said he likes my name because he thinks of the word *sherry* as referring to a colour, more than anything else—the colour cast by light shining through a glass of sherry. After all the comments I've gotten about drinks and wine because of my name, all my life, no one's ever commented on sherry as a colour."

"But your name is Cheri, not Sherry," I said. I was getting

tipsy and starting to feel giddy as my disorientation deep-ened. "You're a dear, not a drink." My voice sounded strange to me, speaking like this with a stranger.

"It's pronounced the same, though. People tend to think in spoken words, not written ones."

I recalled the bottle of what looked like sherry that I'd seen sitting in Richard's cupboard. If Richard had been talking to Cheri about her name, and about the drink, I couldn't help but wonder if he had bought the bottle of wine in expecta-tion of Cheri's visit to talk to him about the Bible. Richard had left me the bottle of Vera wine, after all. He'd also given me the sculpture with the woman hiding her face because he said it was named after truth, like me. Giving thought to Richard's fixation on names made me recall something: I was almost sure that I'd once told him that my mom had always said I'd been named for the Albanian word for *summer*, not for the word *truth*. But he'd given me the sculpture after that. He must have forgotten what I'd told him.

"So you and Richard talked about stained glass?" I asked, wondering how long they had talked.

"We did. And other things—he was a good listener. I told him about my journey in the last few years. My troubles."

"I'm sorry to hear you've had troubles," I said.

"Thanks," she said. "I feel like I'm being cryptic. I'll just tell you. My brother had a head injury a few years ago. He was okay physically but his personality changed. I missed—and still miss—him, even though he's still there. After his acci-dent, I got into a bad pattern with pills and alcohol. I lived with my parents for a few rough years after that. Eventually, I found a support group, though. That's when things changed. I met some people who read the Bible with me and helped me find ways of coping. It's a daily struggle, but I manage. I still drink more than I should, but I'm not ready to work on that at this point. My friends wouldn't like it if they knew, but if they asked I'd be honest about it."

I wondered if Richard knew Cheri's full story. If so, I thought it was strange, maybe even deceptive, that he hadn't told me that they were closer than he'd let on. I also wasn't sure how I felt about him having her over for drinks.

Our server came with the bill. Cheri picked it up and looked at it. She leaned in toward me. "This sounds sudden, but do you mind if we go?" I looked at her, not sure if she meant we should leave without paying. "I mean, I think I'm ready to go, if that's okay. Let's just pay. Maybe we'll split it? Then I'll walk you home." She laughed. I hid my confusion by looking for change and bills in my pockets to cover my half.

The night air back out on the street was damp and frigid, and as we walked, the idea of strolling down the block wrapping up our conversation began to seem impossible, but I didn't want to cut off the conversation. I'd relaxed into her company—the wine had helped. And though I couldn't quite read her, I found her interesting and liked her openness.

"Hey," I said, turning to her on the sidewalk, near Richard's door. "Why don't you come up for a bit? To Richard's place? We can finish our chat and we won't have to stand in the cold."

"If you're sure," she said. "That would be nice."

Upstairs, I let her in and then went to throw both of our coats onto Richard's bed. When I came into the living room, she was sitting on the green couch across from Richard's painting, *Stained Glass Nine*, looking at it.

"Sorry it's so dark in here," I said, and walked around the room turning on lamps. "What can I offer you to drink?"

"What do you have?"

I went to the fridge and inspected the carton of milk and the half-finished bottle of apple juice that had been there when I arrived. I opened one cupboard and saw the jar of instant coffee, and in the next, the bottle of Oloroso del Puerto. I hesitated for a moment, wondering how Richard would feel if I drank from his bottle, and if I'd be able to find a replacement. I decided not to think about it. I couldn't offer her instant coffee or apple juice after she bought me dinner.

I turned to offer it to her, and started: Cheri's hair had changed colour, from dark brown to red. She had lain back against the arm of the couch, and the light cast by the lamp on the end table behind her was falling through the red lampshade, tinting her hair magenta. I shook off the start I'd had and spoke.

"This seems ridiculous," I said. "But all I have to offer you is a glass of what I think is sherry."

She laughed. "The funny thing is that I've been given bottles of sherry all my life, as gifts, for obvious reasons. And I've actually come to like it a bit. What kind is it?"

I passed her the bottle.

"Oh. Oloroso. I had this once, I think. I'd love some, if you're having some."

I poured us each a tumbler full and added some ice from the tray in the freezer, not knowing whether it should be drunk cold or warm. The smell of it was sweet and burnt and made my eyes water and my stomach turn slightly. I sat down at the other end of the couch, and put my glass on the table beside me.

"I wanted to ask you a question," she said. "I can't let myself forget. But first, you should tell me about yourself. I've talked too much."

I started talking and she drank her sherry. I told her about how I didn't know where I was going to go after Richard got back, and about the things I wanted to sell or get rid of to make any move easier. I mentioned the sculpture Richard had given me, and that I'd had to consider selling it, too. And I also heard myself telling her something I'd never told anyone before, that I'd stolen a few things from the department store when I worked there, and still had them in my storage locker. I told her that I thought the management had suspected it but didn't really care. I told her I'd done it on autopilot, and that I'd never stolen anything before.

She paused, looking at me, when I stopped talking, and I could see that she knew I was waiting to hear what she thought. "I'm glad I came over," she said. "I love hearing about people's lives. Yours in particular, I mean, not just in general. I'm happy to have met you."

"What was the question you were going to ask?" I asked.

"Oh, it's about Richard's grandmother. Her art. What do you think of it?"

"It's good," I said. "I like it."

"I like it too. I like her *Water* sculpture. And I figured out why." How did she know about the sculpture in the bedroom? Had Richard told her about it, shown her a picture, or was it somehow possible that she'd been in there?

"Why?" I asked.

"The figure looks strong, even though it's fluid rather than solid. I like that contrast."

"Have you been in Richard's bedroom?" I asked, before I could stop myself.

She looked at me sharply for a second, and then laughed. "I don't like this painting, though," she said, ignoring my question and looking at *Stained Glass Nine* on Richard's wall.

"Why not?" I asked. I felt terrible that I had asked the question about the bedroom. I didn't know why I'd felt entitled to ask it, or why I'd felt the need to pry.

"Because it's nothing like stained glass. The concept doesn't really work. Stained glass changes the colour of light. It takes something that was already there—light—and adds something—colour. This painting takes something that's not there and tries to make it look like it is, but doesn't."

I looked at the painting too, but it was hard to focus. It was so dark in there, and I felt hot. I took another drink of the sherry, my fourth sip, and swallowed it with difficulty, the plummy, dry sweetness coating my mouth. The squares of colour in the painting seemed to shimmer.

"Have you been here before?" I said. "That's what I meant to ask before. I didn't mean specifically whether you'd been in the bedroom."

"Yes," she said. "Once before. But just briefly, to see Richard's art. We didn't have time to talk much. But you know what he told me that day when I came up?"

"What?" I asked.

"He said I reminded him of a woman he'd seen out there, and saw around the neighbourhood after that."

"Did he offer you sherry?" I asked.

"Yes," she said. "Just like you did. But I understand. Everyone seems to want to see me drink sherry. Maybe they just want to see me drink, because of the Christian thing. I know my story doesn't seem to make sense—being religious and being not so clean-cut. Or maybe it does. Anyway, I'm just looking for friends, even though I know people think I'm trying to sell something."

"I didn't think so," I said.

"Maybe I am, in a way. It's what I have to offer right now. Maybe I'll have something else soon. For now, I know from experience that there's a relief in just suspending disbelief. It can see you through. I can't get past this one fact, for better or for worse: for me to get by, I need some kind of film or slide to look through. If I can share that view with someone, all the better. I don't fool myself. I know those people in the recovery group aren't my friends. They just want to project something onto me. But that's not what I'm doing to the people I meet."

"But you don't mind being with people who treat you that way? And you don't mind using their way of talking to communicate with the strangers you meet?"

"I don't do that," she said. "And I'm still here, inside myself, even if people want me to become, or appear to become, something else on the outside—what they want to see. And I don't try to make other people become what I want or expect to see."

She drank the last sip of her sherry. I had another sip of mine, and glanced back at the painting, not wanting to look right at her because I felt like I'd crossed a line. I closed my eyes for a moment, and heard Cheri saying that that she should get going before we both fell asleep. She let herself out, and as I heard her go down the stairs and out the door, I went to the window to see if I could see her walking away down the street. But then I did, and I could—her back was quickly receding from view. I sat back down, feeling that I didn't want to pretend Richard's apartment was my home anymore.

A HEAD FOR WORDS

OF THE TWO WOMEN, CELINA WAS THE WRITER OF THE pair, but she was best known among their acquaintances for having a head for numbers. Mattie, on the other hand, though not much of a writer, had a head for words. Or maybe more accurately, Mattie had a head that was prone to getting words stuck in it, like a spiderweb filling with flies. The words that stuck in Mattie's head, once stuck, would get wrapped up like a spider's flies as she worked on them, until they were iridescent sarcophagi of the flying things they had once been.

For some hours now, Mattie had been thinking over the word *counsel* as she sat in an armchair by a window with a manuscript of Celina's most recent writing project on her lap, in the living room of the dark, perpetually cool house the two women lived in.

Namely, Mattie wondered, as the hours rolled by and she counted down the minutes until five o'clock when she could have her first drink, what exactly is the difference between the words *counsel* and *console*? A few transposed letters; the closing of an open "u" into a sober "o"; a deepening from advice to condolence.

Otherwise, the words were so alike. *Counsel. Console.*

It was raining hard, and the wind made the frame of the house lean very slightly now and then before settling a bit deeper into the black, sodden earth. Mattie wanted a blanket but hadn't yet gotten up to get one. Every few minutes she would pick the manuscript up and read a few sentences before setting it down again, her thumb holding it open where she had stopped.

She gazed out the window, and thought about what it means to offer counsel and what it means to offer consolation. Her thoughts didn't build to any insight. The raindrops slid down the windowpane in the shape of a whorl, as though travelling inside the tracks of a giant thumbprint on the glass.

Celina was sitting at the dining room table looking at her laptop. She was on a marathon Skype call with her ex, Pete, who had recently lost almost all his money because of a series of misguided decisions that he'd said he couldn't discuss in much detail in the email he had sent to Celina requesting the Skype meeting; he'd said he needed to talk to her. Pete was now considering declaring bankruptcy.

"Pete, here's what you need to do," Celina kept saying, before giving numbered lists of advice. Celina was using headphones to talk to him, so Mattie could hear what Celina was saying to Pete, but not what Pete was saying to her.

How fortunate Pete is, thought Mattie, as she carefully tuned out Celina's side of the conversation, so she wouldn't have to share in either the effort Celina was making or the complex misery of Pete's situation. How lucky to have a friend like Celina, willing to spend her day giving expert advice pre-distilled into steps to be executed, the gift of motions ready to be gone through.

"What are you going to do today?" Mattie had asked Celina that morning, in the bright voice that implied that Celina could do anything at all, even though Mattie knew there were many things Celina couldn't do with her eyes the way they were.

"I'm going to take a stab at counselling Pete," Celina had said. "I just can't stand the idea of a problem with no solution. All he needs is his own willpower and someone else's perspective. If I can give him that, I should."

Mattie only enjoyed reading books she had already read before, whose stories and sentences were impressed on her mind, the dirt already turned.

This story of Celina's she hadn't read before, of course, so she was having trouble enjoying it, even though she thought it was good. It was a novella that Celina had been writing and rewriting since she stopped working, called *The Pleasure Garden*. Mattie wanted to be able to talk to her about it, so she was determined to finish reading it.

The Pleasure Garden was a quiet, sparsely written story about a man named Sam, who has recently left his job because of an eye ailment that makes reading impossible. The story follows Sam exploring a huge conservation area in eastern Ontario called Ancient Falls, near the area where Celina herself had been born. In the first chapter, the recently unemployed Sam walks up a winding trail in the bush that he thinks will take him to a waterfall he once found as a child on one of his exploratory rambles. Sam is only fairly certain the waterfall exists. He's never seen the falls on any map. If those falls were there, they would be the real ancient falls, as opposed to the man-made, far-from-ancient "ancient falls" for which the conservation area was named.

An industrialist who lived near the park had transformed the first section of the Ancient Falls park into a pleasure garden, just before World War I began: an opening lawn party was held in the summer of 1913. The crowning feature of the pleasure garden was a man-made, smaller-scale replica of Niagara Falls that was created by blasting a curve of the river with dynamite to create a deep drop and cascading falls, just below a swimming area with its surrounding manicured lawns, stone fountains, and elegant stone steps leading into the river's gentle current. Sam liked the deeper part of the park, past the well-tended walking trails and the plagiarized natural wonder.

"As he walked, Sam noticed spent shotgun shells scattered along the edge of the trail. 'Deer hunters,' he told himself. The shells were rusty. The hunters had been here a long time ago."

That was as far as Mattie had gone with Sam.

Celina was on leave now from her job as a financial analyst for an insurance company. She had moved in with Mattie a few years after she'd stopped working. Celina was about a decade older than Mattie, and they had come of age in adjacent but distinct eras. Mattie wasn't sure to what extent the differences in the zeitgeists that had fostered them accounted for the differences in their personalities. For Celina, career had always been paramount, and to some degree their relationship had been founded on that difference; Mattie's ideal had always been not to work at all. And if she had to work, which she almost always did, then her goal was to work jobs that couldn't define her, that she could walk into in the morning and out of at day's end. This was made possible by the house she had inherited from her grandmother and now lived in. The house meant that her salary as a cashier or a tutor or a freelance writer or some combination thereof was usually almost enough, even when it wasn't.

By contrast, what Celina had wanted in life was to prove that she could be successful within the domain of money; she wanted to be known as a numbers person, i.e., a finance person. She had achieved that. Their friends had always come to Celina with money questions, Mattie included. Celina had advised Mattie on the process of assuming ownership of the house, a process by which Celina also came to assume a sort of share in that house, in Mattie's mind, not least because, as Mattie could admit, in honesty to herself, Mattie needed someone with a head for numbers to take care of things, not because she couldn't, but because she was sincerely loath to.

Because of her financial expertise, Celina—and Mattie, by extension—knew many secrets about their friends, who came to Celina for confidential financial counselling: thus Mattie knew of a secret gambling problem; an online bank account that showed a daily transaction at the liquor store in the amount it costs to buy a single 26-ounce bottle of vodka; and a case of costly emotional blackmail between a man and his former mistress.

"There are three kinds of lives," Celina had told Mattie once. "Public, private, and secret. And every person has one of each."

Mattie knew that in Celina's case, her public life was lived as a financial analyst, but her private life was lived as a writer. Celina's current life was all private: she rarely left the house.

Mattie had always given a lot of thought to what people

care about—not what they would most likely say they care about if asked, but the truth: Celina, Mattie always concluded (when she tried to understand why Celina had sought promotions in a high-status career), must care about power, at least in some form—having it, representing it, or being close to it. Mattie, by contrast, cared about comfort, a by-product of power, which was perhaps part of why she enjoyed having Celina within her sphere. In addition to power, Celina also cared about Mattie. In addition to comfort, Mattie also cared about Celina. Celina had also taken up the job of caring for Mattie some years back. And now Mattie, as she realized, had started caring for Celina too.

Celina had begun counselling Pete on Skype that morning at ten. When Mattie had walked past the table to go to the kitchen to make lunch at around one, Celina was still counselling him.

As she walked past, Mattie had stolen a carefully angled glimpse over Celina's shoulder at the image of Pete on the screen, framed from just below his shoulders, sitting in front of Celina on their dining room table like an animated sculpture, a bust titled *Worry*. His face was slightly distorted in shades of blue and grey against the room he was in, a room full of tall, tangled shadows, as though, Mattie thought, he had been projected from an expressionist movie set designed by him, for the purposes of the Skype call, to emphasize his misfortune. He was sitting in what looked like a study. Books lined the walls behind him; a curtain fluttered at a window-sill and then fell still. Mattie had never been in that house and neither had Celina, but Mattie gathered from what she'd heard Celina saying about the house's location and value that it was somewhere remote, somewhere cheap to live.

Mattie kept herself out of Pete's view as she glanced at him in passing. Was it also raining where Pete was? If so, the rain would match what looked to be his very dark mood. His eyes were puffy with fatigue, and he looked at least five years older than he had the last time she'd seen him. Which, to be fair, Mattie reflected, had been just under five years ago.

It was the weekend their group of friends had rented a cabin together at a pristine rural lake in eastern Ontario, not far from the Ancient Falls conservation area, about an hour away from where Celina had grown up.

Celina had assumed the natural role of host, knowing, as always, how to serve other people: how to make a plan, a budget, a meal, a reservation, a weekend. Mattie had felt out of sorts, with a headache brought on by the humidity and intermittent rain that stacked the air up to the sky in uneasily balanced layers. She lay in bed for most of both days in the room she'd chosen, the room with the single bed for the one unpartnered party; she read a novel she'd read several times before, but not recently enough for it to fail to deliver that particular comfort she sought from a book— the chance to re-enter a familiar but almost forgotten life, to discover not new, but once-familiar places and objects, blurred and changed by who she had become since the last rereading. As she padded around the cabin, around her friends, she found she was thinking about the book and not about where she was.

Late on the second night, Mattie found herself standing at the cabin's kitchen sink with her back to the room, having a glass of water, while all the others were out drinking on the back porch in the warm night air. Their laughter broke in shards over the empty-sounding flatness of the water. Gazing at the kitchen window, marvelling that she could see nothing of the outside, but only the reflection of the room behind her, and her own face, Mattie saw a movement reflected—the reflection of Pete coming into the kitchen behind her, from outside. Then there was another head reflected behind her own: Pete's head overlapping with hers in the glass, against the backdrop of the blocked, pitch-dark night, his breath in her ear in that way that forces hearing and touch together into a sixth sense. Mattie pulled away, pushing him lightly so that he fell back. "You're okay," she said firmly and quietly, as though he had stumbled and she had caught him. She meant: you thought this could keep happening as long it never seems planned, but that's not true.

Mattie picked up Celina's novella again. Sam was still walking.

As he walked, Sam realized it was later than he'd thought; his watch said it was almost four. The cicadas groaned under the pressure of the damp shadows.

From the base of a tree, a blinding glint caught Sam's eye; he approached and saw that it was a side-view mirror removed from a car, placed mirror-side up on a little mound of sticks, rocks, and leaves. He picked it up and, almost automatically, held it up in front of his face. It was strange to see any face, even his own, in this quiet, lonely spot: the sight of even his own eyes made him feel something that he realized was close to social anxiety. He set the mirror back down on the pile of sticks and continued down the path. Sam decided that no matter how long he thought about it he would never be able to work out why someone had left the mirror there or whose car it had come from, so he stopped thinking about it. There was probably no reason at all why that mirror lay on the ground.

He wanted to be so alone that he wouldn't be able to recognize the sight of himself, or even to think.

As his legs found a good rhythm for his walk, his mind, unmoored, drifted to thoughts of his boss, Lucy. At almost every one of their monthly meetings, Lucy had encouraged Sam to toughen up. "Don't be afraid to toughen up, Sam. Every person needs to grow a skin to walk around in," she had said. "You can't just go out raw, with your hopes and fears exposed. You'll never make it." Yet, when she had told him they were accepting his resignation due to the eye problem, Lucy had called upon his inner strength. "You're so strong, Sam," she said, putting her hand on his. "I know you can get through this." For the first time, as he walked, Sam wondered when exactly Lucy had started thinking he was tough enough to rebound from losing his job, even though she had never found him to be tough enough for the job itself while he was working. Had she thought of him all along as a strong, skinless man walking around naked, with brawny muscles exposed as in an anatomical drawing, eyes bulging wide?

No wonder Lucy had so easily accepted Sam's resignation. She had probably been terrified.

Sam decided not to think of the office. He had come too far to go back in his mind. He forced himself to think only of the falls he hoped to find. He pictured the waterfall's foamy torrents, the force of the water driving deep into the dark blue water below, and, above all, remembered the sound, the whiteness of it. But as he pictured the falls, Sam started having trouble not thinking of names he might give them when he got there. He didn't want to name them; he just wanted to know they were there.

Mattie put the manuscript down, startled from this thought by the chime of a clock. She looked up: the clock wasn't in their house, but at Pete's. Celina was still Skyping with him, and had unplugged the headphones. It was five o'clock, at Pete's place and at theirs. Time for her first glass of wine. Mattie silently thanked Pete for the reminder.

She went to the kitchen and chose a bottle of red wine, and got out the corkscrew. She reached into a cupboard and brought out an empty jam jar made of bubbled glass in the shape of a raspberry that tricked her mind into thinking the wine tasted sweet and new rather than dusky and aged. It was dark in the kitchen: they hadn't turned any of the lights on for the evening. The house was illuminated only by the last remnants of daylight, and it had been a dark day anyway because of the storm.

"Pete, I'm telling you, this doesn't have to be as bad as it seems," Celina was saying. Her voice sounded clear and confident in the quiet of the unlit house. Then there was only the sound of the rain. "Pete?" Celina said after a pause. "I promise it's going to be okay." Mattie glanced through the kitchen doorway. Pete's voice answered quietly, and Celina plugged the headphones back in. Celina's back was blocking Mattie's view of the screen. Her shoulders sloped under the soft grey wool of her sweater. Her head was going grey too, mixed with black. Mattie felt tired from Celina's labour.

There was no clear explanation for the change in Celina's eyes. "There's some possibility it could be caused by a concussion," the doctor had said. "Do you remember hitting your head at any point?" "No," Celina had said, shaking her head. Mattie had reached her hand out to make Celina's head stay still. She had had an MRI scan: there was no physical cause for the change in her. But Celina couldn't work, and she mostly stayed at home now. She was still fine with numbers, but she didn't talk more than she had to. Today's money talk with Pete was the most she'd said in a long time.

Mattie filled her jam jar and poured a wineglass for Celina, then lifted both their glasses and the bottle. After she passed Celina, she stretched her arm out and pushed the glass of wine toward her along the table. Pete would only see the full glass appear in Celina's hand when Celina picked it up, and nothing of Mattie. She carried her glass and the bottle back to her chair. She set them on the floor and picked up the novella again.

Sam had stopped thinking of the falls. Instead, he was trying to empty his head completely, to make the sound of the treetops swaying in the warm breeze serve as a trellis for his thoughts to climb on in vaporous vines toward the white sky. He was just beginning to feel calm when he came around a bend and saw a woman walking toward him on the trail.

"Hi," Sam said.

"Hi," the woman said. "Didn't expect to see anyone else out here. I thought no one else knew about this trail but me."

"You, me, and some hunters," Sam said, gesturing toward a shotgun shell on the trail.

"I've seen the shells, but I've never seen a hunter. I've never seen another person in here."

"Are you coming from the river?" Sam said. "From the falls?"

"No, I didn't make it that far today. I want to get back before it gets dark."

The last day of that trip to the cabin, the day after Pete had come up behind Mattie in the kitchen, Celina came into Mattie's room, where Mattie was reading, and asked her if she'd like to go for a drive to see the house she grew up in, at the far edge of the Ancient Falls conservation area and the associated land. The others had gone out on the water in the motorboat. They would be out for a few hours; thermoses of gin and tonic had been packed, a sandy destination in a bay about an hour's ride down the river chosen on a map.

Celina and Mattie had been friends for years, but until that weekend, that day, they hadn't been especially close. It was during the car trip to the farm that Celina opened up.

"This was my dad's farm, but it was his father's farm first. My grandfather was exempt from military service during World War II because he was a farmer," Celina told Mattie as they walked down the treelined country road that led to the lot where the farm had once been. They came to a stop in front of what was now a large empty yard with a big oak tree that had a rope hanging from one branch (the remains of a tire swing, Celina said) and a stone wall that lined one side of the property.

"His contribution to the war was to collect scrap metal," Celina said. "He would pile it against that stone wall until the pile would get half as high as the house, and then a man with a big truck would come load it all in and drive away with it, so that it could be melted down into metal for weapons. That was, obviously, before my time, but my mom told me about it so many times, and showed me the pictures, and it became like my own memory. Growing up, I loved playing on that wall, because I would find odd bits of metal hidden between the stones or buried in the ground at the wall's base that had been left over from the scrap pile. A horseshoe, an iron bar, a steel circle. A twisted bit of aluminum. Each of the pieces of metal I found looked like a letter of the alphabet to me, and I laid them all out on the lawn and worked on it until I made them spell something. Finally, I rearranged them enough times that they more or less spelled the words *Back through*. It could only be a message, I thought. A message planted in the wall during the war by a spy. Maybe my grandfather himself had been a spy. It was clear enough to me what it meant. I had to go back through the forest behind our property. I was officially forbidden from going into that forest, but I had to go."

"So, did you ever go back there?" Mattie asked.

"I did, but the only interesting thing I ever found was a small waterfall. Still, there was some kind of danger there that my mom would only hint at. She would get irate and shut things down if us kids talked about it as a mystery or a game."

Celina and Mattie walked together into those woods that day. About a half-hour in, they came to a grassy clearing and, on their left, saw what looked like an old road, a trace of one heading back toward the main road they had started from. A rusty wheel protruded from the ground. Alongside it, another bent piece of metal stuck out, another wheel. In the centre of the two wheels, scraps of cloth and rubber protruded from the dirt. It was a baby carriage that had sat there so long that it had slowly sunk into the ground.

"I remember finding this before," Celina said, "It's been here forever. It terrified me. I thought the wheels were the rear tires of two ancient bikes, side by side, and that the kids who had ridden them long ago had been swallowed by the ground while they rode, the ground closing back up around them, leaving only the two back tires unburied. Everything back here seemed to vibrate with meaning in those days. But in the end, I never found anything that interesting back here."

When Mattie and Celina returned to the cabin, everyone else seemed quiet, sunburnt and a bit drunk, and they all packed up to leave in near silence. Pete and Celina drove off in their car, the other couples in theirs, and Mattie in hers, having made an excuse not to carpool but to drive up alone. On the highway, Mattie found herself driving along at first behind Pete and Celina's car and then beside it. She stayed beside them but they didn't notice her, and she didn't lose them the entire way back to the city.

As Celina and Pete pulled up into the entrance to the underground parking lot of their building, Mattie parked across the street, got out of the car, and then slipped into the underground lot. Mattie saw them lugging their bags into a glass elevator. Back outside, she followed with her eyes as the glass box stopped at the seventh floor. She sat in her car for a few moments. She watched the lights come on one by one in one of the condos, a big corner unit overlooking the lakeshore. The condo had been bought in large part with Celina's money; once it was invested in the condo, Pete had thought of it as his money. But he hadn't fought to keep what he felt was his, because he didn't want anything coming out in court that Celina didn't already know, about his relationship with Mattie while he and Celina were still married.

Pete could only see, would only ever see, Celina—and

not Mattie—in the small square view of Celina's home that his screen showed him, an excerpt of her new life with no context visible beyond its cropped limits. Mattie thought of those other, distant squares that held a past configuration: first, the car Pete and Celina drove in, ahead of her; then, the elevator they took up to their condo; finally, the condo itself, with its huge windows: three boxes of glass, each holding, suspended, the life Celina and Pete had shared. Pete's money—or what he'd thought of as his money—belonged to Mattie and Celina now. But Mattie didn't care about the money; she cared about Celina, and what little she could understand about why Celina had chosen to care about her.

Mattie gazed out the window of the house she lived in now with Celina, which sat at the edge of the city, far from the city's lakeshore and the building where Celina had once lived with Pete. Celina was still talking to Pete. Mattie had come to the spot in Celina's manuscript where Celina had switched from type to handwriting, because she found the screen too hard on her eyes when she was writing. Mattie wondered if the screen on Celina's laptop was bothering her eyes now, as she talked to Pete. Mattie's own eyes were beginning to become strained from reading, partly because of Celina's handwriting, and partly because she was starting to feel like a stranger in the world of Celina's story.

ANYA'S PAINTING

WHY DO WE EAT BIRDS' EGGS BUT NOT REPTILES' EGGS? It's a question Anya used to ask when we would go walking at the bottom of the city by the river, watching the cormorants whirl in the rainy air. Now, when I walk by the lake behind the condo building I live in—my new home, in a new city, without Anya—I'm reminded of her question. The birds are sleek, silent. Collapsible when they land, like black umbrellas. "But they're dinosaurs," as Anya would say. "It's as plain as day. If we are what we eat, then we're a lot less like we are than we think." That's how Anya talked, sometimes not so much *to* me as *beside* me.

I recently moved from one city to another, and into a lakefront condo tower named Shoreline Terrace, where I live alone. I've been getting to know a new geography.

I'll admit that in my first weeks in the building, I was dazzled by all the frills of condo life, and the extent to which the residents seemed to take them for granted. Anya had warned me: "Just because you have nouveau money, don't think nouveau riche is going to feel natural."

I think Anya found the Dickensian twist of fate that intervened in our lives to be in poor taste. My grandmother passed away and left her condo to me, her only grandchild. It meant I would have to move across the country if I wanted to live there, but I was ready for a change anyway. When this happened—completely unexpected, but, to me, the best of all possible news, the end to the cold, to Anya's shoplifting—Anya got interested in travelling. She got a job teaching at a high school overseas and left the country, instead of crossing the country with me to go to what I'd hoped would be our new home.

With her gone, what else was I going to do? I had to move somewhere. But I find the condo residents strange.

For instance, I quickly became convinced that some residents aren't even aware of the storage available to us, down there in Shoreline Terrace's expansive, dry, quiet basement, with its broad rows of stalls. Whole households of furniture could remain for years down there in packed-away units. But the lockers sit almost entirely empty, small forgotten rooms with walls made of raw boards.

Except for my storage locker, that is. I know it's weird, but I'm going through an adjustment. Some of my furniture just didn't look right to me placed in the condo itself, so I put the misfit pieces in the locker. A chair. A space heater designed to look like a fireplace—complete with moulded flames painted orangey red with smoky licks of charcoal grey (which I was able to run in there with the help of an extension cord). And Anya's painting. It was a perfect triangle of furnishings, as it happened: a little room completed by the portable window of the painting, which I hung from one of the two-by-fours that structured the space. I took to sitting down there. Maybe I liked it because it was so warm down there, not only because it was close to the building's boiler, but also because of that reliable old space heater. Anya and I had bought the heater years ago for our old, always-freezing apartment, where we lived back in the other city, before fate stepped in and made an expatriate of Anya and a condo dweller of me.

That old apartment was beyond cold. Once, Anya had placed a thermometer on the dresser beside my bed at night. It told us that it was twelve degrees in there. We took pictures of the thermometer, had them developed, and wrote the words "please note" on the back above our signatures. We sent the pictures to our landlord with stamps affixed to the upper right-hand corner like postcards. He claimed he never received them. That fake fireplace got us through our first winter together.

Our cat, Prometheus—who had dragged himself into our lives from some invisible urban wilderness one night, scratched up and bloody from a fight—got his name from that fake fire. He never let us touch him, but he would sit with almost-shut eyes beside the heater all day, all night, all winter, entranced. "Our copy of Prometheus's theft from the Gods," Anya said. "Stolen again, this time from Walmart." The space heater was one of her major shoplifting victories. We guessed that the poor cat had never known fire or its warmth before, stolen or not.

The last time Anya and I had talked had been shortly after I'd moved into Shoreline Terrace. Trying to embrace my new home, I stood looking out my condo's window over the water as we talked. "You could stay with me here when you visit next. You'd like the lake," I told her.

I listened to her stories. Her job was supposed to be temporary, but she had quickly become blended like paint into an unending night of a life there: an impressionistic slurry of cabs; food eaten near dawn with strangers; names for bands and books thought up and forgotten; eye-numbing piles of assignments to mark all day, every day.

But there was something wrong with her phone or with our connection; her voice was crackling and faint, and I could only hear fragments of what she was saying. I pictured telephone wires at the bottom of the ocean sinking deep into the silt of the sea floor, cutting into the mud and being swallowed by billowing and settling sediment below the swimming paths of eyeless fish. Does it work like that? Did it ever? Or was it a satellite being knocked by the debris of a fragmenting asteroid?

Growing weary of trying to make out what she was saying, I told Anya that I needed to get off the phone. I didn't tell her that I wanted to go sit in my storage locker and feel the building above me sitting like a giant creature roosting on the rocks, gazing out over the lake, me its unhatched egg.

That's what I did do, and what I started doing a few times a week, thus leading to the evening in question, when I sat in the storage space drinking a beer and considering calling Anya again. I gazed at her painting that was hanging in front of me. It was starting to bother me.

Anya was a good painter, sometimes by accident and sometimes on purpose. Once, at our old place, she found a bunch of old paintings on the side of the road set out with someone's trash. She took them home and painted over the canvasses one by one in our kitchen. She would sit at a chair with a canvas in her lap, leaned against the edge of the table, her legs in black tights splayed out straight in front of her in an easel-like "v." The cat would walk through and leave a trail of coloured paw prints behind him on the newspapered floor, each print fainter than the last until they disappeared, like the creature who had left them had levitated into the air.

Her "portraits," she called them. But there were never people in her paintings: only places. And sometimes animals, usually with their backs turned: an owl flying toward the brown light in the sky above a parking lot, or a coyote limping across an empty expressway, its head low and facing away, its fur moulting from its hide in bunches. She said the animals weren't symbols. She wouldn't explain much beyond that.

The one piece of hers that I'd kept and brought with me to the condo was the painting that I had hanging in the locker. It was the only one I could remember her ever doing that had people in it—though they weren't prominent. A house was the main subject, a dark house among stands of trees at night. The whole painting was dark except for the light seeping through the seam of the ajar front door, and a small, glowing window with a silhouetted cat sitting in it. Behind the cat, in the house, were the silhouettes of two people, one with arms held up, as though captured in animated conversation. But tonight, for the first time, it struck me that the exchange looked less like a conversation and more like an argument. And I'd always thought the cat in the window was facing outward, toward the painting's viewer, but I realized now that it was crouched low with its head turned to look inside, directly at the people in the house, as though startled by a noise.

A change in perception can register on the brain like a flash at the edge of our vision: it seemed that it was only just now that the cat in the painting had turned its head.

I decided to get out of there and clear my head, stretch my

legs. It was a nice fall night anyway, a good night for a walk to the lake.

I have a usual place I like to sit by the lake: the firepit. Another perk of condo living, not strictly owned by the building owners, but used by the Shoreline Terrace residents as a place to roast marshmallows or hotdogs. I sit there almost every afternoon, looking out at the horizon.

If I sit with my back to the building, right on the shore, I can imagine I'm not in a city at all. There's an island out there in the lake, to the west, near the end of a long, thin spit of land that curls into the water. At a quick glance, the island looks like it's connected to the spit—the last joint of a finger pointing away from the city, advising exodus. But if you look closely, you can see the brief stretch of sky where no trees rise up.

When I first noticed the island, I wondered if I was the only condo resident who knew for a fact that it was out there—but I had no way of knowing. Until a night quite recently, I had barely spoken to the other residents. I could hardly count as conversations the commiserations about condo fees or the weather that I didn't participate in, but overheard in the lobby or in the elevator (me smiling sympathetically, sliding by, looking at my hands like they had instructions written on them).

That night, after talking to Anya and looking at her painting for too long, when I left the basement and went outside through the back, lake-facing doors of the building, I went straight for the water, past the firepit, down to the water's edge.

Stepping among the rocks and close to the gently lapping

water, I saw something orange in the reeds: the nose of a small tin boat. I uncovered it.

"Hey!" a voice said behind me. "Hey! Boat thief, stop!"

A man in a tuxedo jacket came up beside me, stumbling through the firepit. He had a white silk scarf around his neck, the kind Fred Astaire would wear. Under his dark hair, his face was greenish. It could just as well have been a symptom of his obvious drunkenness, but it was clearly face paint.

"Don't look so scared! I'm only kidding. It's not my boat. I've never seen it before. Now, we haven't even properly met." He put out his hand. "I'm Dead Frank Sinatra."

"I was thinking Fred Astaire," I said.

He sat down by the non-existent fire in the firepit and put his hands out, as though warming them. He pulled them back in and hung his head in his hands. Slowly, he let his fingers drag down his face, smearing the makeup into stripes that revealed another layer of makeup.

"Ah, this condo," he said, his eyes looking through his fingers, his lower eyelids pink and watery. "It's an endless night. Do you want a drink?" He reached into the pocket of his jacket and pulled out a green bottle, unopened. A shade of green that meant gin, the medicinal taste of juniper already on my tongue.

"Sure," I said.

"You can drink first," he said, handing it to me.

"No," I said. "You first."

Somehow the issue of who would drink first displaced the question of whether or not I would drink at all. As long as he drank first, I thought, it would be okay. I would watch for signs in him that there was anything other than gin in the bottle. He drank first, and passed me the bottle. I took a swig, and handed it back to him.

"Have you ever noticed how much everyone in this building resents the condo fees we have to pay? Why do they resent them? In exchange for the fees, we get things. They even built a path that leads from the terrace door down to the water. The landscaping is well done. It keeps you company, even when you're alone. Is that not worth a few fees? Maybe the residents who begrudge the fees don't want the feeling of company, I try to remind myself. Maybe they just want to work all day, party all night, and rollerblade for an hour along the lakefront in the windows of time left over."

He drank again, and looked at me. "Don't look worried. Do you want to go back up?"

"Up where?"

"Back to the roof. To the party."

"I didn't know there was a party."

"I assumed you'd come from there. Yes, there's a party on the roof, tonight, all night, every night, all summer, into the fall. We had a tropical theme for most of August. Now that fall is in the air, we've switched over to Halloween season. Most of us have run out of costume ideas, and it's not even October yet. We're in a dead-celebrity phase. This should last until Christmas, when we'll move inside and set up a tree in the rec room. You'll know the season's changed when you hear bells." He stood up. "Are you coming?" he asked.

"Yes, I guess so," I said. Since my arrival, I'd felt different from the other condo residents; it was a comfortable sense of difference, and not one I saw aligning with the weirdness of my new companion. But I had to at least try.

We walked up the path to the back terrace and through the glass doors to the elevator, a silent, green-carpeted glass box that swallowed us up and slipped like a beam of light up the shaft to the top of the building. Frank leaned his forehead against the glass, gazing out over the view of the lake, the dark expanse of black water invisibly joining with the sky. Out in a westerly direction, where I thought the island must be, I thought I saw smoke rising grey into the air.

When the elevator opened, it was into an empty, carpeted corridor, with chairs and furniture and artificial-flower displays. Frank slipped through a door, and I followed him into a dark ballroom, across which I saw him gliding toward a pair of French doors on the far wall, his white scarf fluttering and catching the moonlight as he threw them open, the warm noise of unknown voices surging up and into the silence like uncorked bubbles.

The roof was covered in grass, dark, soft, and wet-looking, so that I felt almost like I was stepping into water. Overhead, coloured lights were strung in rows about a foot above head-height. Flimsy tables were set up under the lights and littered with bottles and empty glasses. Women swayed on high heels that sunk into the turf under the weight of draped beads, long wigs, and furs, haphazard costumes thoughtlessly assembled but still disconcerting.

A group of people in leather motorcycle jackets encircled a woman. She stood on a tabletop, her body wrapped in black-and-white fabric, a cat mask covering the top half of her face. She was swaying almost imperceptibly, I thought. Maybe she was about to sing. The men appeared to be awaiting entertainment.

"She's the goddess of the condo," said Frank.

Two arms appeared on either side of Frank's face and locked his neck in a chokehold. A man's blond head poked around Frank's, laughing, and he threw Frank down onto the grass. The blond man was dressed in a wrestling outfit. Frank drunkenly flailed his legs, wrapping them around the wrestler, but he was pinned. They stopped fighting, and just lay there, looking like they thought they should laugh but didn't have the energy.

Not knowing what else to do, I joined the biker people around the table and watched the swaying woman. As I watched her from under the lights against the black sky, I started to wonder if she was even moving—if I was seeing her shift and flicker from side to side, or whether the light reflected by the shiny fabric she was wrapped in was playing tricks on my eyes. Yet she appeared to move. The black of the fabric and her mask blocked out a negative space in the sky with no stars, the triangles of the mask's ears like distant, silhouetted mountains. I became aware of music, a high sound, reedy and booming. The dappling of the coloured balls of light in green, blue, orange, and red swayed as the string of light was blown. Then, it stopped: I could only hear the voices around me, the clinking of glasses and the broad, diffuse sound of the wind. Sensing that her performance had ended, the people around the table started wandering away.

The woman stepped off the table. She extended her hand to me and smiled under her mask. "Welcome," she said. "You're new here. I'll show you around."

Wordlessly, she walked me back through the ballroom, and into the corridor, where she glided to the elevator and pressed the Down button. In the elevator, I started to say something, small talk, but she was peering through the glass toward the lake. "Just a minute," she said, putting up one forefinger to pause me.

When we got outside, she ran ahead of me toward the firepit. She looked back at me. "Thank god," she said. "It's still here." She leaned down and parted the reeds away from the boat.

"I was planning on going out on the water tonight, and I hate going alone. You could come."

"Sure," I said. The prospect was irresistible. Truth be told, I hadn't left the condo in a few weeks, and I'd always wanted to go out on the lake, to look back at my new home from a distance, to see the lights at night. I didn't understand who exactly this woman was, but I couldn't say no.

She pushed the boat half into the water and I got in the front, sitting with my knees on the floor. She slid the boat the rest of the way in and stepped in, settling herself on the rear seat. The low churn of the oars in the water launched us and we were slipping out onto the lake.

The wind was cold lifting off of the black lake and I couldn't see much ahead of me in the dark.

"How long have you lived here?" I asked.

"I've always lived in Shoreline Terrace. My mom raised me here—you might have heard of her, she was a famous painter. She died when I was sixteen, and I never left. They call me the condo goddess because no one here can remember a time without me."

"Where are we heading?" I asked. But I knew. We were quickly approaching the little island at the tip of the point.

We slid up onto the sandy beach of the island and got out of the boat. The island was tiny. We sat on the edge of the island's shore and looked back at Shoreline Terrace. It was dwarfed by the city lights behind and around the building, and the cluster of other condo buildings around and behind it. The whole city looked like a massive, distant ship docked for the night, the lights the ship's windows, with Anya visible in none of them.

Acknowledgements

Thank you to those who read early drafts of these stories: Malcolm Sutton, Ellie Anglin, and Matthew Strohack.

And thank you to those who helped me to shape the ideas in these stories through their support and conversation: Michelle Andrus, Cara Fabre, Phill Pilon, Robyn Hartley, Kamil Rzymkowski, Meagan Snyder, Paul Barrett, Marcia Morse, Fiona Foster, Lisa Rumiel, Janet Friskney, Sarah Whitaker, Ann, Al, Dan, Caro, and Andrea. And thank you to my teachers: Jacqui Smyth, Mary di Michele, Mikhail Iossel, and Elizabeth Hanson.

Unending thanks to Margaret Anglin for her constant support and for all the quilts. And to Jerry Anglin, for being who he is and for sharing his love of *Nine Stories*.

And finally, thanks to Jay MillAr and Hazel Millar for all the tireless and inspired work they do, to Malcolm Sutton for being an exceptional reader and editor, and to Stuart Ross for his excellent copy-editing work.

Colophon

Distributed in Canada by the Literary Press Group:
www.lpg.ca

Distributed in the United States by Small Press Distribution:
www.spdbooks.org

Shop online at www.bookthug.ca

Designed by Malcolm Sutton
Edited for the press by Malcolm Sutton
Copy-edited by Stuart Ross

BOOK
PRODUCTION
WAR ECONOMY
STANDARD